Metal Earth

Metal Earth

by

ANNE ALDERSON

Flyford Publications

Copyright © Anne Alderson 2015
First published in 2015 by Flyford Publications
Hill Court Farm, Grafton Flyford, Worcester WR7 4PL

Distributed by Lightning Source worldwide
The right of Anne Alderson to be identified as the author of the work has been asserted herein in accordance with the Copyright, Designs and Patents Act 1988.

All rights reserved. This book is sold subject to the condition that it shall not, by way of trade or otherwise, be lent, resold, hired out or otherwise circulated without the publisher's prior consent in any form of binding or cover other than that in which it is published and without a similar condition including this condition being imposed on the subsequent purchaser.

All the characters in this book are fictitious and any resemblance to actual people, living or dead, is purely imaginary.

British Library Cataloguing in Publication Data
A catalogue record for this book is available from the British Library

ISBN 978-0-9928061-0-1

Typeset by Amolibros, Milverton, Somerset
www.amolibros.com
This book production has been managed by Amolibros
Printed and bound by Lightning Source

Prologue

Around four and a half thousand years ago a race of Europeans crossed to the shores of Britain, bringing with them items the British Natives had never seen before: worked copper, tin, lead and gold. When metal ores were discovered in these islands, the populace, prospering from both farming and metal manufacturing, became wealthy enough to form a hierarchical society. Those from the top strata of the communities would have been the owners of the beautiful bronze jewellery, ceremonial swords and spears, and gold ornaments made in that era which archaeologists are still discovering. The people of the times believed that when they died, the souls of these great tribal leaders, whose remains are found today buried under cairns of stones high in the mountains, watched over and guarded them as they lived and worked below in the valleys. They were known as the Wise Ancestors.

The Bronze Age, as this time is known, was not an age of peace and tranquillity in Britain. Most people worked back-breakingly hard; lives were short and full of disease and pain, and they lived under the thrall of the Spirits of their world – weather, seasons, nature, fertility, and most important of all, water – be it rivers, wells, lakes or ponds. It is believed that the hoards of bronze jewellery, weapons, even everyday cooking utensils, found today in the bottoms of lakes and rivers were placed there as votive offerings, cast into the water to appease the Water Spirits. Priests of the society would have been key players in the communities, appearing to be in touch with both the worlds of Spirits and of Human beings, and the ordinary people may well have joined together as a community to erect the stone circles that dot the uplands of Britain today, believing they could aid the priests in their important work.

Towards the end of the Bronze Age the weather took a serious change for the worse, and for some years Britain endured only cold and rain, summer and winter alike. There was widespread flooding, soils were washed away, and without sunshine food would have become short and life precarious. Much of the population died or fled. Those who remained faced isolation, fear and famine. It is not known for certain why the weather changed so dramatically, but it has been suggested the Icelandic volcano, Mount Hekia, which erupted at that time, triggered a long-lasting blanket of cloud over Europe; others believe a comet or meteorite passing close to the earth interrupted weather patterns.

The story takes place on the Lleyn Peninsula in North Wales, towards the end of this time. Iago's tribe, living by the sea, and within reach of the copper mines on what is now The Great Orme's Head, would have had access to fish, seabird eggs, seaweed and shellfish in addition to what food was left on the land, and could have survived in the watery world. Evidence from the land has shown that when this difficult period of history was over, people who had knowledge of working a new and different metal, iron, were entering Britain. Iron was stronger and could hold a sharp edge for longer than bronze; it was a more powerful metal, and bronze weapons would have been no match for it. It would have been regarded as mysterious and awe-inspiring.

Chapter One

The hill was perfectly rounded, its summit crowned by a tower, built from the stones of the ground and painted ochre red. Viewed from the village it had the shape of a woman's neat breast, but the man standing alone next to it three thousand years ago felt only awe as it loomed over him. The walls were as straight as ancient knowledge and magic could make them, a reminder of all the treasures the Earth held; and just as the hill and its tower could be seen from all points of the surrounding land, so he could look down on to his native green countryside and the grey forbidding sea. The rain, flying in the harsh June wind, pinned his hair to his head and his clothes to his body, but he was a young man of stature, and stood erect against it. His name was Anarhys.

The name of the Hill was Mynedd Carngwch. It was a holy place, and Anarhys had climbed it to ask for a blessing from the souls of the Ancestors who built it before setting out on his journey. "Please, Fathers," he prayed aloud into the wind, "intercede with the Spirits to make the sunshine return to our land, to make the grass grow and the corn ripen so our tribe does not go hungry. Please watch over us on our undertaking to bring home bronze sickles for harvesting the barley." He stood respectfully for a moment, allowing the Ancestors to hear his words, then he turned to face down the Hill. Living as he did on the Lleyn Peninsula, he viewed a landscape already deforested, and as wild and desolate as today. Through the blanket of rain he could just see his village; it was half hidden in a valley which opened into the sea, the few roundhouses standing staunchly against the relentless downpour. He could make out the enclosures built around them for domestic stock: small horned cattle, primitive sheep, and two stunted brown ponies which would provide meat for the villagers through the next bitter winter. The sheep supplied course wool for clothing and the cattle were milked until they dried up and became thin from cold and hunger. Then they too would be slaughtered for food.

On the track at the foot of the Hill Anarhys could see the two tiny figures of his friend Cavan and his sister Yrwen waiting to start on their way with the three cows. The cattle were impatient to move out of the shrieking wind and into the lee of the Hill, and Yrwen, Cavan and the black herding dog held them with difficulty. For a moment Anarhys thought of his father, Iago, asking him to undertake the task of taking the livestock to the bronze factory on the Gogarth Headland to exchange for bronze sickles. It was a risk letting the cattle go, but Iago believed there was a chance that bronze, with its mystical properties and sharp edges, would cut the barley more quickly than flint. He hoped it would give the tribe a better prospect of feeding his tribe, but Anarhys had known it was with a heavy heart he had sent his son, daughter and Cavan on their way with the precious animals.

Yrwen was shouting urgently up to him but Anarhys couldn't hear what she was saying against the crying of the wind. He could see the animals were ready to break away, so guessing the meaning of her empty words he hurried down the Hill, through the dank heather and the squalls. By the time he reached the track where they were waiting the leading cow had set off at a brisk walk, her head lowered into the wind, her back shining with water. The other two followed pushily behind.

"What kept you up there so long?" Yrwen said stormily as he reached her. "You could see the problems we were having holding them." She was wet and tired. The leather cape covering her shoulders and back was already heavy stiff with water, and she was having to walk much too quickly, almost run, to keep up with the little herd. Anarhys looked at her. She was thin from undernourishment like them all, muscled by the work of tough farming, but with intelligent eyes fringed with long eyelashes in its worn familiar face, her fair hair scraped back, tied with a strip of bleached hide and tucked into her cape to keep dry. She did not look happy. "I didn't want to come anyway. How long will we be away from home?" she added, still irritable, and hurrying alongside the cows to keep them on the track.

"A few days, no more," Anarhys shouted over the wind to her. He was filled with guilt as well as anxiety, but he had to keep this from the other two, especially Yrwen. He wanted to confide in Cavan but wasn't sure whether he should. The cattle steadied their pace as they passed the lee of the Hill and turned into shelter, and the little party slowed, but only enough to breathe easily. They marched into the pass leading north, the ragged grey mountains rising into the mist on either side. The rain was relentless. It had rained for weeks. Narrow waterfalls streamed from the hillsides, the grass was sodden, the mountain pass up to their ankles in mud. The dog slouched along behind, looking as though he wanted to go home, but keeping the cattle moving forward. Anarhys was up ahead, leading the way and keeping the pace. Cavan and Yrwen walked as an outriders, one either side of the little herd and a little back to keep it moving. The leather bag on Cavan's shoulders was heavy already and he had cut a straight hazel stick to help him balance. He was taller and leaner under his clothes than Anarhys, a man who could run quickly, but who found long gruelling labour hard work. Yrwen walked angrily.

Although the mountains were sheltering them now from the west winds, conversation was impossible in the heavy rain. They walked with hardly a word spoken between them, becoming wetter and hungrier as the hours went by. It was much later that Anarhys called a halt by a sheltering rock before the mountain pass opened out to the coastal lowlands.

"We'll have to stop" he shouted back briefly. The hound dropped to the ground, and Yrwen stumbled over and sank down with it, leaning against it for warmth. The weary cows, which at the start of the journey had been impatient to move on, turned their tails into the wind and lowered their heads to forage for grass. They were tough animals, smaller, stockier and with thicker hides and coats than today's cattle, and capable of living outside in all weathers. Even so, fast travelling was telling on them. Anarhys and Cavan looked at them from under the brims of their dripping leather caps.

"Why do we have to go so fast?" Cavan asked, brusquely, brushing away raindrops from his face. "Look at them. They're exhausted They won't be fit to trade if we go on like this. And it's making Yrwen so irritable she'll make our lives miserable."

"I know, Cavan," said Anarhys shortly. "Get your back bag off and let's have a break for something to eat." The leather thongs that held the bag in place had been cutting into Cavan's shoulders and he took it off thankfully, walking over to Yrwen. Carefully opening the bag so the rain didn't pour in, he reached inside, took out some flat grey bread and handed it over to her. It had been baked from barley, ground, mixed with water and a piece of sheep fat, and cooked by a fire. With it came two strips of cold cooked meat. They didn't look at all appetizing and Yrwen took them silently. She felt like throwing them on the ground in temper, but was too hungry to do anything but eat. The dog looked at her longingly.

Cavan turned back to Anarhys, and passing him some food, said, "So, come on, Anarhys, tell me why you want us to travel so fast? What's the point of getting to the mines so quickly if the cows finish up exhausted? They should be looking their best to get some sort of deal for them, not worn out from racing up to the mine."

Anarhys ate away silently for a long time, asking himself whether it was wise to share his concerns, but deciding in the end that it would be a relief to talk to Cavan. They had been friends for most of their lives and trusted each other. "All right, I'll tell you then," he said finally. "But you probably won't believe a word I say. I don't know if I believe it myself. It's the Iron People."

Cavan gave a shout of laughter. "The Iron People? Don't be ridiculous. There's no such thing!"

"Well I don't know whether they exist or not. But there's a rumour that they're starting to work their way up the coast towards our village, attacking settlements as they go. Last time I was in the next village they were talking about it and taking it pretty seriously. If it's true, and they come this far, they'll see the smoke from the factory at the copper mine on Gogarth Headland and attack that too. We need to get back home before that happens."

"It's nonsense to believe in the Iron People," Cavan said easily. "They're a non-existent, mythical race. Even if they are real they've never come here before. Why should they now?"

"I don't know, Cavan. I suppose they're short of food, just as we are. I suppose they come along the coast because it's easier for them than across the land." He felt the hair stand on the back of his neck and shivered unhappily, trying not to let Cavan see. He was not nearly as certain as his friend that the Iron People were a merely mythical race. According to the stories they were men to be feared. It was said that they sacrificed men, women and children; they drank strange brews which enabled them to go through the Gates of Death to meet their Ancestors and return to the physical world again; and they used weapons forged from a metal so powerful it would crush their own bronze swords and spears. Nobody knew where they came from. He shivered again at the thought.

"It's all nonsense. When I was little my father

frightened me with stories of them, but now I simply don't believe it." Cavan threw the last bit of bread to the dog who leaped up for it, leaving Yrwen sprawled on the ground. She stood up, frowning.

"Yrwen doesn't need to know," Anarhys muttered, looking away. Cavan looked surprised. Yrwen was a stoic young person who probably wouldn't believe that the Iron People were on their way, even supposing she thought they were real. Parents and older siblings frightened children with tales of this monstrous race of men, but most people in those times were working much too hard for their survival to pay serious attention. Still, for Anarhys' sake, he kept quiet.

"The cattle must have more time to rest," said Yrwen obstinately. "They're hungry. Their feet are getting sore. The little one's udder is full and she needs milking before we move on."

"You're right, Yrwen," agreed Anarhys, and Cavan looked at him curiously. Anarhys didn't usually placate his sister. He thought there was something else going on that Anarhys hadn't him told about, but he shrugged off the idea. Knowing Anarhys so well he guessed that if there was something he wasn't saying it would come to light between them soon enough.

"I'll take some milk from her," went on Yrwen interrupting his thoughts. "She hasn't long calved. Please hold her, Cavan, she might be feeling tetchy."

Cavan gently took hold of one of the little cow's horns. The cattle lived among the village huts and were used to being handled and Yrwen was able take milk from her with no trouble, talking to her softly as she always did. Anarhys removed his leather cap to catch the milk, and stood bare-headed in the teeming rain. They worked together efficiently.

"There isn't much," said Yrwen. "She's hungry and tired." She might have been talking about herself, and she was glad to take a warm drink. The milk was more satisfying than dry bread and meat and she felt better straight away, less angry, less tired. Anarhys saw this in her face and felt relieved. Cavan took a drink, then passed it to Anarhys. Afterwards he washed it out in clean water which lay on the marshy grass. Despite his saturated hair and clothes, Anarhys began to feel more positive.

"We'll go for another stretch, then stop for the night," he said.

"Where?" asked Yrwen.

"We'll find somewhere," came back the answer. Where indeed? Anarhys thought. He had not been on the track leading north to Gogarth for years, and could hardly remember it at all. After an uneasy rest, huddled together at the base of the rock, they moved on again, out of the protective shelter of the mountains, and into the lowlands. There was a break in the downpour, and as it lifted they could see they were travelling not far from the coast, parallel to the sea. It was not azure blue and uplifting as it had often been when he and Yrwen were children, but threatening, cold and grey under sombre clouds. It had looked like that almost every day for years.

"I don't like leaving the mountains," Anarhys said to himself. He glanced anxiously over his shoulder at them as they receded into the mist. "Our wise Ancestors are up there, buried under the stone cairns on the mountainsides, close to the Spirits of the Air. They look down on us, watching and protecting us, but I shouldn't think they can see us now we're so far away. I don't trust the lowlands. I don't know what the tribes living here are like, or where the wolves might be, and I can't get away from the wind." He looked around warily all the time as he walked. As the son of the village Elder he considered himself responsible for this journey and felt accountable for the safety of Yrwen and Cavan. He was probably only half right in this: Yrwen judged herself as well able to take care of herself and the cows, and Cavan had a habit of watching him from afar with a discerning eye.

★★★

The first major river the party had to ford was their first setback. Familiar with living in the mountains, and crossing gushing little becks which they could often jump over, this was a different thing altogether. It was swollen with rainwater gathered from the mountain streams, and was roaring, brown and frothy, towards the sea. It was about twenty feet wide. Had they been travelling along its length instead of wanting to cross it, the water would have been their ally, directing their steps and providing them with food and drink, but that was not the path they needed to take. Its Spirit was trying to turn them back in an obviously hostile way.

"The Ancestors will help us," said Anarhys at length, as the three of them stood together on the bank looking at it speculatively. He didn't really believe his own words. As far as he knew the Ancestors had been left behind in the mountains. "We must ask them what to do." He looked across at Cavan hopefully.

The river raced on noisily, blocking their way. Cavan

moved a little way away to stand alone in the landscape. He had an innate understanding of spiritual matters, inherited from his father. He listened to the Ancestors' voices as they whispered sibilantly to him in the wind, and he frowned in concentration, trying to make out the words. After a while he understood that they wanted him to walk upstream. He took himself off with loping strides and a short time later came back to the others with news.

"There's a crossing place further up," was the information, and he took his hat off and waved it in the direction he had just come from. His hair was instantly plastered wetly to his head. "And there's a village on the other side, I think," he added.

Chapter Two

Perhaps the River Spirit had helped them after all. If there were people at the settlement they might be peaceful. In former times, when the weather had been good, there would have been a thousand people living in this part of the countryside, thriving on livestock breeding and arable production. When the weather had changed for the worse, fifteen years before this story, Human lives were shortened through disease and death, and many families had left the area to search for better lives. Whole villages of traditional thatched roundhouses and outbuildings on Lleyn were now abandoned. The few tribes that remained, scattered along the coast, were bound together by necessity.

Anarhys looked at his friend. He had known him for as long as he could remember. Cavan had moved into Gwrtheyrn village with his father when they were both very young, Yrwen just a baby. There had been a sizeable group of children among the families then, who should all have grown up together, but during the hungry years some villagers had died and others left to look for something better, taking their children with them in the hope there might be a better future for them. Iago, Yrwen and Anarhys were the only three left of their family: two brothers and their mother had died and gone to be with their Ancestors. Iago was now the tribal Elder.

Their woollen clothes were old and drab, thought Anarhys, glancing at Yrwen. There had been a time when it was fun for the women to make new clothes, and experiment with dyes, competing to see who could wear the brightest colours. At festivals and tribal gatherings they had washed their hair, brushed it to make it shine, and worn polished coloured stones to match their skin and eyes. The men wore cloaks fastened with shining bronze pins, and with trimmed beards and hair looked confident and smiling. Now the main necessity of everybody was simply survival, and if bronze sickles instead of a flint ones could help them in this, it was what they had to have, even if it meant selling half their cattle. Again Anarhys looked back longingly to the mountains he had just left; the mist had evaporated and he could see them in the distance, ranging black against a darkening sky. For a moment he imagined that perhaps they could all turn round and go home to them. Then he remembered his father. He could not possibly let Iago down.

"Lead on then, Cavan," he instructed, pushing the words out of his mouth almost against his will, and he followed his friend, turning back along the marshy bank of the racing river. The three cows, glassy-eyed with fatigue, followed him, and the black dog continued to pad along behind, his tongue lolling from one side of his mouth. Their track veered away from the river after a short time, and the sound of the rushing water diminished. When they came upon the it again further upstream it had indeed become wider and shallower. A stunted alder tree, its roots hanging in the river, grew over it on a bend where the brown water rattled over a stony bottom, and there was a shallow sandbank on the near side. As Cavan paused, the lead cow pushed past him and scrambled down to drink.

It would have been tempting to make a camp here for the night, even without much shelter, and wait until the next morning to attempt the river crossing. Cavan was right that there were people here; the smell of wood smoke told them roundhouses they could see on the far bank were inhabited. As they watched, two yellow dogs appeared from the village. They were barking for all they were worth, but Anarhys couldn't hear them for the deafening river. They were followed by a single male figure.

Anarhys felt uneasy as he eyed this unknown person over the river. He had met many of the Lleyn people through trading or at gatherings, but they were away from their own countryside now and he didn't recognize him. He knew that in foreign countryside such as this acutely hungry men would steal or attack for food, and whilst he had been on this journey before he had never visited the villages on the way. He had no way of knowing whether the man he was watching was hostile or friendly, and the marshy grasses and dwarfed trees on the flat lands around them held no friends either, Three unarmed people with valuable livestock were vulnerable in strange lands. He gave a thought to the small gold disc in his money belt, pressing into the skin under his clothes.

More people had joined the unidentified figure on the opposite bank of the river, but there was still nothing to tell the travellers whether they represented danger or goodwill. The sun was almost touching the horizon, and if they were going to cross tonight it had to be immediately. Anarhys stood for a time thinking about his options. The temptation to turn back to Gwrtheyrn village nagged at him, but he told himself he must not stop at his first serious hurdle. If he went home without even crossing this river their efforts would be seen by the whole village as failed. Both he and his father would be compromised. He himself could never become the village Elder.

I suppose we shall have to attempt the crossing, he thought, in the hope that they and the cows survived it. (He never considered the dog.) If the people on the opposite bank are hostile we might be killed or the cows stolen from us. If, on the other hand, they are friendly we might be given shelter for the night. But if we camp here for the night where there's no shelter I shall still have to make that decision in the morning. The thought of warming himself by a fire was almost overwhelming to Anarhys.

Yrwen's thoughts were mainly for the cows. The current in the middle of the river was fast, and they would probably have to swim, but near the banks they could wade. They would be washed downstream for a short time, but if they could get their footing before the river narrowed again they could make it to the far side. All they could do was take the risk and see. The milking cow would go dry from the shock of the cold water, but she had not long calved, and would come back into milk if they could find her some decent food. A cow with milk on her was worth more than a dry one.

Cavan stood very still and listened to his Ancestors. They were telling him to go forward into the waters. He had a momentary vision in his head of a tree trunk further down the bank, lying into the river from the far side, with loose branches stacking up against it. Taking courage from this he took his bag from his back, ready to cross.

"Let's go," pronounced Anarhys, finding all the willpower he could muster, and stepped behind the cows. Persuading them into the water was going to be the first problem. He took a last glance at the setting sun.

They stationed themselves behind the herd, waving their arms and shouting, and at last the lead cow stepped nervously into the rattling torrent. Anarhys watched as the others pushed in behind her, and as the last one lurched forward he saw Yrwen catch hold of her tail. With the other hand she caught the dog by the loose skin behind its head, and cow, dog and Human headed out into the current together. Pushing his bag onto his shoulder and grasping his hazel stick, Cavan followed. The figures on the other side watched. The yellow hounds on the far bank had stopped barking.

As the sun tipped the horizon Anarhys stepped into the river. He saw by the bobbing heads that the cows were now swimming, and Yrwen was towed with them. Then the shocking cold and the roaring of the water took over his senses. The waters pulled vigorously at his legs, and without a stick to act as a third leg he found it difficult to stay upright. A sudden surge of water swept him off his feet. The last thing he glimpsed as the current took him downstream was the cows scrambling up the muddy bank to safety, and unfamiliar figures waiting on the other side to reach down to Yrwen and help her out.

Putting every effort into keeping his head out of the water, Anarhys was resigned to the futility of shouting: nobody could hear him over the roar of the brown water, and it was impossible for anybody to reach him. It was useless to attempt swimming to the bank as the force of the water was too strong, although he caught sight of people running down the river bank alongside him as he was swept along. There was a terrific thud on the back of his head and he felt himself go limp, followed by a moment of absolute calm in which he surveyed his life and felt his Ancestors close by. Then the sensation of river water thrusting against his body forced him to realise he was still alive.

Not only alive, but caught up amongst twigs, with the river rushing past him. Hardly daring to grasp them in case they broke and sent him back into river, he turned his head. They were branches all right, and they had been heaped up against a small tree trunk that was lying part way across the river They were slippery with river weed, and rotten with age, but they were a tentative security. The River Spirit had given him a punishing test, but was now offering a chance. In the growing darkness he could see somebody edging carefully along the fallen tree.

"Take hold of the branches, Anarhys!" the figure was shouting as loudly as he could over the sound of water, and at the sound of his name Anarhys felt some strength come back to his body. He turned his head again to look at the branches, and offering a little prayer to his

Ancestors that they would take his weight, reached out and caught at those nearest his hand.

"I'll be fine," he managed to splutter back in answer, hoping it was true, and tested the strength of the decaying branches by pulling his body gently towards the bank. Some of them broke softly away in his hand, but he managed to make a stride's length before realising to his relief the other person was standing on the fallen tree trunk and holding a larchpole out to him. Taking a deep breath, he clutched at it with one hand, and before the river could carry him away grabbed it with the other. He concentrated hard on keeping his face clear of the water by keeping his head back, and felt himself being dragged slowly through the water before human hands caught his arms. Afterwards he couldn't remember being tugged up the marshy bank and helped into a sitting position on the grass. He simply felt his woollen clothes hanging heavily on his body, saturating him; his body was shuddering with cold, and he found himself no longer at the mercy of the River Spirit.

"Thank you," he managed to say through teeth chattering as never before, and looked up at his rescuer. He saw a face older than his own, darkened by woodsmoke and lined with worry, but the eyes appeared friendly and concerned. He felt a rough blanket being wrapped around him by an unseen hand. He pulled himself to his feet, shivering violently, and found himself lurching along a path by a field of corn leading towards the roundhouses. He had time to notice that the corn was growing no better than their own at home, before he was ducking under the doorway of the biggest of the roundhouses. Even though it was summer there was a central fire giving off heat and light; it drew its smoke up to the roof where it dispersed through the reed thatch.

As he entered the house the interior came alive to him. In the sudden semi-darkness Anarhys became aware of the firelight flickering on the stone walls, the crackling of the flames, figures rising to their feet and coming towards him – among them Yrwen – being helped out of his soaking clothes and having dry blankets wrapped tightly around him.

"Anarhys," Yrwen said, somewhat crossly. She was worried about him. "Are you all right? We thought you'd gone. Why didn't you use a stick to cross like Cavan?" He could see that she too was swathed in a brown rug which was woven with pale patterns, but he was too cold to be surprised by this.

"I'm all right, Yrwen. Where's Cavan? What about the cows?" As his eyes focussed he glanced around, and there was Cavan standing by him, looking incongruous, wrapped in rugs.

"We all made it across the river, and so did the cows," Cavan answered quietly and carefully, "although one of the cows is lame and probably won't get to Gogarth." As Cavan said this all three felt an invisible balance between them return. With his ducking in the river, Anarhys had felt that he had lost face with the other two, but as the present state of affairs was reported to him he knew he was being acknowledged as the expedition leader again. Despite his tiredness he stood as tall as he could.

The man who had pulled Anarhys from the river sat down on the rushy floor, gesturing for them to sit with a wave of his arm. "I'm Mabin, tribal Elder of Ddu Village," he started; "This is Caersws my brother," indicating a younger man to his left, "and this is my wife Menith." There was a small clay pit by the fire, with a stew cooking in it, and Menith kept it simmering by dropping in hot stones which she fished from the fire. She nodded to her visitors but did not smile.

"Anarhys, Cavan, Yrwen, from Gwrtheyrn Village," said Anarhys, using the same protocol. "And we are indebted to you."

"Yes indeed," replied Mabin. "And now we can also give you hot food, and your cattle may rest in our enclosure for the night."

Anarhys felt a moment of unease and remembered suddenly the precious gold disc. He felt for the money belt under the blanket. To his relief it was still there, although their clothes were arranged round the fire, steaming in the heat, so Mabin must know about it. "You are very kind," he returned formally, wondering whether Mabin was planning to take advantage of them in some way, or ask them to do something in return for their safety. He looked around the roundhouse for clues as to what it could be, but there was nothing. The yellow hounds were lying up against the wall stretched out and dozing, but did not look threatening. There was the usual clutter of cooking utensils, food and bedding, but no weapons. Then he added, "Is there anything we can do to return your kindness?"

"There is, Anarhys," said Mabin. There were a few quiet minutes while Menith handed round bowls of hot fish stew. This was a feast in those hard times. Again Anarhys wondered how they could repay the favour, but like the others he took the food thankfully.

"You are travelling to Gogarth for bronze," went on Mabin, and it was a statement, not a question.

"What makes you say that?" asked Anarhys cautiously.

"Where else would you be going to along this route with livestock, except to trade there?"

A pause, while Anarhys realised there was no point in denying it. "Yes," he said eventually. With his stomach filling up he was beginning to feel better and more hopeful.

"Then this," said Mabin, "is what we ask of you."

Chapter Three

There was a stillness in the roundhouse. The fire purred and crackled quietly in the hearth; smoke pushed its way out through the roof, blackening the wattle walls and finding its acrid way into eyes and noses; clothes steamed in the heat, and the yellow hounds stirred in the shadows. There was a smell of wet fur and wool.

The sounds and smells took Anarhys back to his family's roundhouse in Gwrtheyrn, and with a pang he recalled his father. In the good days before the rains came Iago's prestige would have been displayed by his clothes and bronze sword shining at his side, but after fifteen years of fighting for his tribe's survival he stood before Anarhys in his worn tunic, the grey beard ragged on his chest and dark hair streaked with white. This was all that remained of his status of age and wisdom. He had committed Anarhys to this journey.

"Anarhys," Iago had said to him, his lean face wrinkled with anxiety, "Gwrtheyrn Village has twenty-five inhabitants. It's difficult keeping the village together. You know as well as I do that if we don't get enough sun to ripen the corn properly again this year there won't be enough food to see us all through the winter."

"Yes, Father," Anarhys had replied brightly, and with the enthusiasm of youth, "but we've done everything we can to improve things We asked the Ancestors up on the holy Hill to help. We asked the Earth Spirit grow the barley. We even gave the Water Spirits an offering to stop the rain. You were there. We presented the last of our bronze jewellery to the Sea. It'll be fine this year, you'll see. The sun will come out this summer as it used to, and we'll have a massive corn harvest. Enough for everyone in the village, and some left over to sell."

"No, Anarhys," Iago had said, his voice tired with cynicism. "Listen to me. We've waited for a decent summer for fifteen years. Each year we do everything we can to please the Spirits, but it never makes any difference. Every summer the harvest is worse and there's less to eat."

Anarhys, about to contradict him, had reached out to put his hand on his father's arm. As he did so he was silenced by how thin it felt. They were all gaunt, every person in the village. They would be scrawnier still by the end of next winter if there was no harvest. So would the precious animals, their providers of meat, milk and clothing.

"If more men die we can't sustain the tribe," Iago had said gently. "Don't you see? We need to do something more. However much we sharpen the flint scythes they aren't good enough. Supposing for a moment there was enough sunshine. If we could reap the barley more quickly we'd get more stored before it spoiled in the rain. We need new blades for the sickles. If they were made of the glittering bronze our Ancestors would be pleased with us and help intercede with the Spirits. I'm too old for the journey. In any case, I'm needed here. You, Anarhys, must to go to the bronze works at Gogarth and trade three of our cows for good bronze sickles."

Anarhys remembered the anxiety he felt as he heard those words. There were two reasons he could see for not going to the bronze factory. First, losing three of the village cows would halve their herd. Secondly, the trip north to the Gogarth Headland would be difficult enough, but dealing with the bronze smelters at the copper mine would be a formidable task: they had the reputation of being people of deep mystery, and tough to do business with. He could have asked if somebody else could go instead of him, but simply couldn't, even though the mission sounded almost impossible. "And," Iago had added, "Yrwen can go with you."

Anarhys remembered mumbling "Yrwen! Why on earth Yrwen, Father? She'll never keep up. And she always argues with me."

"She can keep up easily, and she's the best person to take the cattle," Iago had said, "and there's another reason." Iago paused, waiting to catch Anarhys' attention. "You will take Yrwen with you to Gogarth, and find her a husband while you are there."

Anarhys's world had stood still. His sister sent away to belong to the wild Gogarth bronze traders! It was an unbelievable idea. She'd never survive being married into the rough Gogarth tribe, she was far too rebellious. He wanted to argue but found himself unable to speak: his tongue wouldn't form the words.

"She must go, Anarhys," Iago had said. "If she gets

pregnant here our tribe can't support her, and any babies will die. She's old enough to leave and live with another tribe. There's wealth at the copper mines. She'll be better off there than starving here with us."

Anarhys had looked at his father's grey face, took in his old clothes, and had a moment's inkling of the sacrifice he was making in sending his daughter away.

"Yes Father," he grunted, and there was a moment's silence between them. Then Iago had said:

"Cavan can go with you. But there's one more thing I want to tell you. There are rumours of Iron Men invading our lands."

"Oh that old story! I didn't think the Iron Men existed," Anarhys had cut in quickly. "The whole thing's made up, isn't it?"

After a moment Iago had answered, "Perhaps, Anarhys, but stay alert in any case. If they do come, other tribes will try to warn us by lighting beacons on the mountain peaks. Keep checking, and if you see either warning fires on the mountains, or Iron Men's ships on the sea, head for the protection of the valleys inland and take cover there. They are sea-faring people. If they come it will be by sea and they won't go far from it. They will camp by the coast. They'll be looking for iron ore. They know how to make weapons from it that would make any of our bronze swords quite useless. Not that we have any left. We couldn't fight them."

"Well you seem to be sending me at the wrong time then," Anarhys had retorted with a touch of levity. "What good will Yrwen and I be to you, hiding in the valleys from a race of imaginary people that we were frightened by as children? We're not children now." He stopped talking as a fleeting uncertainly caught at him. "Surely you can't be serious, Father?"

"Last thing. Not only am I entrusting you with my daughter," Iago had continued, ignoring him, "but also with this. We have two pieces of gold left. They are all our remaining wealth from when times were better. Take one of them with you as a safeguard in an emergency. But only use it in a crisis, Anarhys. Only in a crisis."

Iago had held out a tightly woven money belt. Anarhys took it and opened it. Inside was a small disc, leaf-thin and gleaming. On one side a fine pattern was imprinted around its circumference; inside this it was perfectly quartered by delicate lines. At its centre were two minute holes. He emptied it into his hand and it had felt cold and heavy, glittering dully in his palm as though there was a force in it that he did not understand. With a lurch he had remembered his mother wearing it when he was very small; she used it to fasten her blue cloak, and it shone lustrously against the colour. He had said, "Yes, Father," and tied the money belt round his waist in acceptance of the task. It had stayed there ever since, squeezed against his stomach.

The feel of the money belt jolted Anarhys back into the present. Feeling strongly that he had been somewhere else for the last few minutes, he looked round Mabin's round house to bring himself back to the present. Nothing had changed. Five others were still sitting round the fire – Yrwen and Cavan – wrapped in their woollen blankets – and three people he hardly knew – Mabin, Menith, and – what was his name? Caersws? All eyes were on him, waiting. Again he touched the money belt with his hand. It was amazing it hadn't been swept away in the river or stolen from his body. He could feel the disc pressing coldly into his skin.

Mabin was speaking. "Like you, we have animals but not much corn. We also need to take livestock to Gogarth for trading. If you, Caersws and my son travel together you will make a bigger group and it will be safer for everybody."

"Travel together?" Anarhys asked incredulously. "How do we know we can trust you? We don't know you. You might take our cattle and leave us with nothing. What about Yrwen? I mean, how safe would she be with two of your men?"

"I can look after myself," came Yrwen's voice from the other side of the fire. "Stop trying to protect me, Anarhys. And the cows will be quite safe with me."

"We could go outside and discuss it together," Cavan suggested. Anarhys was annoyed. He was supposed to be the leader on the expedition, and here were the other two telling him how things should be run. He wondered how to turn the conversation to put himself back in charge.

"Don't forget we would be taking risks too. We don't know you either, and there are three of you," said Mabin. "It's quiet at this time of year as far as the work goes, but even so I can only let two people leave the village. Caersws and my son could be useful to you.

Anarhys stood up to give himself status. "How?" he asked.

Mabin remained seated. "Caersws worked at the copper mines on Mon for a time before we needed him here, so he has some knowledge of bronze," he said. "He won't be fooled by the Gogarth traders. They have taken so much copper from the mines that they are having to dig deeper for it. They are even sending little children down for small seams of ore. They might be tempted to put too much tin in the alloy which would make the bronze brittle. Or if they haven't any tin to put in it would be too soft. Caersws will know if the bronze is a poor mixture. If he's with you when you're trading he can advise you."

Anarhys bristled at the suggestion that his group were ignorant about bronze. "I'll discuss it outside with my friend. Come on, Cavan," he said curtly, walking quickly to the door.

"This is the deal," Mabin cut in quickly as the two younger men reached the door. "We have two ponies to be traded up on Gogarth. Dara is a good herdsman and he will go with them. "You take Caersws and Dara with you and bring them back safely. We keep your lame cow here. When you come back with my brother and son your cow should be sound, and you can continue home to your village with her.

Anarhys paused for a second to take this in, then marched on through the doorway. It was difficult to move in a dignified way dressed in only a blanket, but he did his best. Cavan followed, and so did Yrwen, piqued that she hadn't been consulted and determined to be included in the discussions. There was a porch where they stopped together and looked out into the night. As they stepped into darkness they saw the usual moonless, starless sky above them, but for the moment the rain was holding off. The black dog appeared by Yrwen's legs. Boldly she went back into the roundhouse to ask for something for him to eat.

Anarhys was still shocked from his time in the water. "If they were going to steal the cows from us they would have done it by now," he said, shivering and pulling the blanket closer. He rubbed his arms.

"We don't know that they haven't taken them. We haven't seen them yet and we don't know where they are," reasoned Cavan.

"But they wouldn't have rescued me from the river if they were intent on taking the cows. They would have let me drown."

"They might have done if they thought you could be useful to them."

"How could I be useful to them?"

"Well, if you had something they wanted."

"Like what?" Anarhys asked suspiciously. He hadn't mentioned the gold disc to Cavan, so surely he couldn't know about it.

Yrwen reappeared in the doorway, the black dog by her legs and a piece of bread in her hand. It leapt up and took the food from her hungrily. She looked at it with compassion. It was as underfed and ribby as they were. She had a clear understanding that humans and dogs had always had a mutual relationship. Men did the organising, which they were good at, and dogs did the scenting and running, which they were good at, and they worked together. Domestic stock, on the other hand, were food. Cattle were special, being both food and status symbols, a double blessing. And in all cases, so long as people looked after their animals properly, the animals would look after the people.

"Are the cows all right?" she asked. She dodged back into the roundhouse again, her blanket billowing out behind her, and demanded a torch. Inside, Caersws pushed a pitched branch into the fire and handed it to her as it lit. She carried it carefully outside. "Over here," she said to Anarhys and Cavan. They saw Mabin had risen to his feet in the house and was watching them shrewdly from the doorway. There was a stockyard built up against the roundhouse. Mabin's village cattle were out at summer grazing but the three red Gwrtheyrn cows had been corralled here, and Yrwen was gratified to see somebody had thrown a little pile of hay down for them.

"They look all right," Cavan said.

Anarhys held the torch up and Yrwen climbed the enclosure fence and went over to them. She checked the young heifer's udder, then looked over all three of them. They turned their bony heads towards her, surveying her with dark trusting eyes, and she could smell their warm milky scent and honey-flavoured breath. The oldest cow had a noticeably swollen knee. Yrwen put the palm of her hand on it and felt the fierce heat issuing from under the tight skin.

"She won't be coming with us tomorrow," she said, straightening up. "She must have given it a massive bang in the river. But there's no blood, and she's standing on it, so it can't be broken. It's a sprain, I would say."

"Two cows left," said Anarhys. "Not so many to trade. We were hoping to come back with a really good sickles. It'll be hard to get what we need with just two."

"We can't take her," Yrwen repeated stubbornly.

"No, we can't," agreed Anarhys. He wanted to ask Cavan what he thought about Mabin sending two of his people along with them, but Cavan was being very silent. They stood together in the torchlight, the blankets billowing pathetically around their legs in the night breeze, and it seemed to him that Cavan and Yrwen were waiting for him to say something. He had a decision to make – an intelligent decision. And then he had to stick with it.

"If we refuse," he said at last, "Mabin will finish up keeping our cow. And if they really helped us with no ulterior motive, say stealing from us or even killing us, we have done nothing for them in return. I owe Mabin my life. But if we let two unknown men come with us we risk them attacking us on the way. We haven't seen Dara and have no idea what he is like. On the other hand, there are three of us and only two of them, so it could be more risky for them than for us, and they may genuinely need our help on the journey. There is also the risk that Mabin won't let us take our cow back with us when we get back to his village. Even so, I say we take Caersws and Dara." He had a sudden sense that the Ancestors were close to him, nodding wisely. Having made up his mind he was immediately filled with lightness and resolve.

"We don't really have an option," Yrwen pointed out. "Let's just hope Dara doesn't turn out to have two heads or three arms. He'd frighten the dog."

Cavan laughed, the first time they had heard laughter for some days. "He'd frighten me if he looked like that," he said. "Shall we go back in and tell them what you've decided, Anarhys? I feel foolish wrapped in this blanket, and it's beginning to itch. Our clothes might be dry by now."

Anarhys went back to the round house with the torch,

and ducked under the doorway. The sharp smoke hit his nostrils immediately, but he had lived with the smell all his life, and paid no attention. He thought he had taken on the cloak of leadership at last, and sat down with his sister one side and his friend Cavan on the other. Then he gave the pitch branch to Caersws to return to the fire. Straightening his head, he said, "We agree to you terms, Mabin. We three and your two men will travel together to the Gogarth Headland, each do our trading, and return here together. Then we take our lame cow home with us."

Even in the flickering gloom, Anarhys could see that Mabin's face did not change. There was no smile of relief on his lips or gleam of cunning in his eyes. The black dog had followed Yrwen through the doorway and was making itself small behind her, but there was no comment about that either. Mabin merely nodded.

"When do we get to meet your son, Dara?" Yrwen asked, thinking to herself that this was a question Anarhys should be asking.

"Tomorrow morning," answered Mabin. "He will treat your lame cow before you go, and she will be much better by the time you all return."

"How will he do that? Her leg's badly damaged."

"You'll see him at work in the morning. For now let's all get a good night's sleep. There are two more days of travelling before you get to Gogarth."

There was movement in the round house. Menith finished clearing away the remains of the meal. Caersws damped down the fire with peat turfs. Most of them went out to glance at the sky and relieve themselves, and other figures came in through the door like shadows to sleep. Thankful that it was not winter, Anarhys lay down in his blanket on a bed of heather and let his mind wander. The river water had battered his body and he ached badly. He felt more in control of his expedition now that he had made the decision to take Mabin's men along with him, and it eased his mind. But every time he started to fall asleep the sound of the rushing river water and the fear of drowning came over him again. He lay awake for a long time listening to the night sounds – the other bodies breathing and moving as they slept, the swish of a breeze gusting over the roof outside, a scuttle of vermin against the outside wall. Only when the early morning sun came up and the birds welcomed it with a dawn chorus did he relax at last into sleep. A short time later Cavan was shaking him awake.

Chapter Four

Inside Mabin's roundhouse it was dark. The curved stone walls and thatched roof were blackened from years of smoke, the fires left a film of soot on the stone floor, the scarlet glow of the embers on the central hearth showing through the peat made the sods look as black as pitch. When the other shadowy figures pulled themselves to their feet Anarhys, Yrwen and Cavan rose with them. They searched round the fire, found their clothes, and pulled them thankfully over their bodies. Cavan's bag had dried out along with their clothes, but the food packed inside it for the journey was spoiled, and the two yellow village dogs and Yrwen's black hound breakfasted well on it. Their leather outer clothes were as stiff as planks to the touch when they dressed, but it was raining yet again, and there was nothing for it but to bend and stretch them about in an attempt to soften the fibres, and pull them on too. As Anarhys shed his blanket to dress he quietly slipped his fingers into his money belt and felt for the gold disc. He felt its outline under his hand bring back more childhood memories of his mother in her cloak, her blue eyes reflecting its colour. He offered the Ancestors a word of thanks for its safe keeping.

It would be good to get out to greet the dawn, thought Anarhys, never mind the rain. As he stepped through the doorway and into the daylight he saw that the clouds were so low they had formed a thick mist throughout the village. He breathed its damp droplets, and it condensed on his hair and clothes, leaving a shining dew behind. There would be no hope now, he thought with a small inward smile, of seeing any beacons burning on the mountain tops. In the foggy morning light the houses and shelters of the settlement had a look of permanency in the landscape, as though men, women and children had been living like this since time began. He walked over to the enclosure where his cattle had been held overnight. They emerged cautiously out of the mist towards him.

Mabin joined him at the fence. "Good morning, Anarhys," he greeted him. "I hope you slept last night after your adventures in the river yesterday."

"Yes I did, thank you," Anarhys lied, standing straighter and determined to appear at ease, in charge of his own matters and unperturbed by his frightening brush with water the previous day. In the daylight Mabin appeared to him more clearly than yesterday: he had grey-flecked hair almost down to broad, bony shoulders and light eyes in a worn face which was weathered and blackened from smoke. Most people Anarhys had come across in this part of Britain were fair, and occasionally they had startling blue eyes and a pale skin, as his mother had had. When Caersws joined them a moment later, Anarhys was taken aback to see that Mabin's brother didn't have this colouring: he had remarkable russet-coloured hair and tawny eyes, unlike anything he had ever seen before.

"Then come and meet my son Dara," went on Mabin, as Anarhys tried to prevent himself staring at Caersws in fascination. "Then we can give you food to take for your journey. You must realise that Dara has unusual gifts, and he's very candid, almost to the point of rudeness." Then he added, "But accept him for what he is. He'll be able to help you."

"I'll just wait for Cavan and Yrwen," said Anarhys, not too bothered about unusual people, so long as they weren't violent. Every settlement had at least one, and each had his own useful place in village life. But he was concerned to know what his second travelling companion would be like. When Yrwen and Cavan arrived, Mabin led them all to a small roundhouse set on its own. Stopping outside he called out Dara's name.

This is peculiar, thought Anarhys. Why didn't Dara sleep in Mabin's house? And why don't we just go in out of the rain? The house was dark inside. It had no porch, just the doorway, in which a figure suddenly appeared. At first sight Dara looked like any one of them, with a brown woollen tunic and trousers, waterproof hat and cape, and leather boots with toughened soles – quite small in stature, perhaps, but then, thought Anarhys, he might not be very old. Most of the villagers were up now and moving round the village, but the five men and Yrwen, standing together in a tight knot, were paying attention only to each other. Caersws stood at the back of the group, and he and Mabin looked searchingly at their visitors. Yrwen, Cavan and Anarhys looked curiously at Dara. Dara gazed back, unabashed.

He looks normal, thought Anarhys.

Mabin said "Dara, these are the people who will travel to the Gogarth Headland with you and Caersws." He related their names.

"Good morning, Anarhys. Good morning, Cavan. Good morning Yrwen," Dara recited with a nod to each as though he was committing each to memory.

"Good morning, Dara," they replied, and there the conversation came to a graceless stop. Anarhys took a closer look at Dara. He saw that he had the same unusual hair and eye colouring that Caersws had, but where Caersws' hair was dulled with age, Dara's, which fell to his shoulders, was copper-coloured, and his eyes were grey-green, and ringed with black. And he had been right about the age – Dara was young; he still had a rounded boy's face, not the lived-in face of a man, and he had the slight build of youth.

"Perhaps, Dara, you would look at the lame cow for these people," Mabin said to him. "Her knee is badly swollen."

"Yes I will, Father," replied Dara, and led the little group of people to the pen where the cattle were held. He stood very still at the perimeter fence for some time, saying nothing, and then, with hardly a sound, slipped between the rails and moved noiselessly towards the three creatures. Yrwen went to follow him, but Mabin stopped her, saying "Wait a moment, Yrwen."

"But she's my cow, I don't know what Dara's going to do to her," she remonstrated.

"I know, but wait," said Mabin, and Yrwen paused reluctantly, clearly annoyed.

Dara seemed entirely oblivious to all around, except

the little beast in front of him. He approached the cow's shoulder on its lame side in a curious sideways movement, with his head turned in such a way that he was only looking at it out of the corner of his eye. His hands were hidden inside his tunic and the animal regarded him benignly, watching from prominent, luminous eyes that could see all around. Anarhys became aware that Dara was making sounds – not speaking, as Yrwen would to animals, but with a low humming that could hardly be heard over the sound of the fine raindrops dripping on the ground. After a while he turned his head slowly and quietly to call Yrwen over to join him.

They stood together in the pen. Dara closed his eyes and ran his hands down the cow's forearm. When he came to the hot and swollen knee joint he placed his palms over it – not touching, but holding them a little way away, and leaving them there immobile for a several minutes..

"There's nothing broken," he said to Yrwen.

"I know that," she replied stiffly. "She couldn't stand up if there was."

"It's just really badly sprained. She might have twisted it when she was climbing up the river bank. It'll heal quite easily if it's rested," and he brought from inside his tunic a small leather bag. From it he took five tiny slivers of bone, sharpened at one end. Holding one between his thumb and fore-finger he pressed it gently into the hide just above the knee, until it pierced the skin. Yrwen was alarmed, but the cow did not flinch. He left it there and put the other four fragments in beside it until five bone pins were standing out of the skin over the cow's knee. Leaving them he walked to the front of the animal and again held the palms of both hands out to the cow, this time just above her chest. Still he did not touch her. After a while the cow's head sank slowly towards the floor, the gentle eyes ringed with long lashes half closed, and her breathing became slower. She even gave a relaxed little sigh. She was almost asleep. Yrwen watched suspiciously.

A little while later Dara gently stood back and, with infinitely small movements, took the bone pins out of the cow's hide, putting them together in his hand, then touching her shoulder with his fingertips. "It won't cure her immediately but it will help her heal," he said to Yrwen, without looking at her.

Unusually, Yrwen didn't know what to think or say. She had never seen anything like this done to animals before. She glanced over at Cavan and Anarhys, but standing as they were a little way away they hadn't been able to see what Dara was doing. Dara slipped between the rails and came out of the pen again. They all watched as he buried the bone shards in the wet ground. Still standing in the enclosure, Yrwen said, "If somebody brings me a container I'll take some milk off the milking heifer."

A beaker was fetched from inside Mabin's roundhouse. There wasn't much milk: all the animals were tired and hungry. "Let them have some grass," said Mabin, and the rails were opened to let them out. Yrwen followed. Despite the lack of sunshine there was some good June grass, and the cows grazed it greedily, the rain falling relentlessly and unnoticed on the coarse red hair of their backs. The milk was shared out gratefully among Yrwen and the five men as they stood together. All of them looked in silent appreciation at the cows as they did so. Cattle were their saviours. Before the Rains all the local tribes had been intelligent and committed breeders and dealers of domestic animals, and prime among these were the cattle. These days they were well aware that their very lives depended on the remains of the great herds they used to own.

The mist still hung around, distorting sounds and images. It didn't seem a friendly place until Mabin said, "Come inside for breakfast before you leave," and Anarhys went after him into the roundhouse, Yrwen and Cavan following, and the black dog sloping in behind. Yrwen found its presence comforting. She felt uneasy in this unfamiliar village, especially when she thought back to the way Mabin and Caersws considered the strange-looking boy's peculiar treatment of the cow quite normal. She had never seen anything at all like it before, and thought the whole thing bizarre. Even odder, Dara had disappeared again. If he was coming with them why wasn't he here in the roundhouse with them now? As they sat down again she stole a glance at Cavan. She trusted his judgement, and she saw that he seemed quite relaxed, even smiling to himself a little. She had always been aware that Cavan sometimes knew what was going to happen before it actually did so, and far from being disconcerted by the idea she valued it. Well, if he wasn't worried by events then she wouldn't be either, she thought. Cavan saw her puzzlement and gave her arm a reassuring squeeze. She was taken by surprise. Not many people did that to Yrwen.

They breakfasted on smoky tasting barley bread and smoky flavoured cheese. Berries and haws would have been a welcome addition, but hedgerow food wouldn't be ready until autumn. In any case, even when the season for it came around there would be very few; as a result of the wet weather there were hardly any insects around to pollinate the flowers. It was a disturbing thought. As they ate, Mabin said, "We can send a little food with you but we can't spare much. You'll have to forage for yourselves along the way. It's only for a few days."

"Thank you," said Anarhys. Menith took Cavan's bag and returned it with flat bread and dried fish. They were ready to go.

Yrwen took her dog and went to fetch the cows from their grazing. They came reluctantly, and she and Cavan penned the lame one. They took a look at the swollen knee, and decided between them that the swelling was as big as ever, despite the boy's strange treatment of it. When Yrwen put her hand on it, however, she felt certain some of the heat had gone.

"Here, Cavan," she said, "feel this." He reached out his arm and felt the place, the palm of his hand searching for the telltale heat of inflammation.

"You know, this feels cooler than it was before. I suppose it could be healing on its own, but it's quicker than you'd expect. Perhaps Dara's done it some good after all. What did he do, exactly?"

Yrwen explained. It sounded unbelievable to them both.

"Do you really think it's something Dara did?" she asked him quietly.

"Yes, I think it could be."

"What do you make of him?"

"Not sure. Bit odd. Give him time, Yrwen. Look, he's coming. And look at the pony he's got with him!"

Yrwen turned her head to see what had made Cavan exclaim, and saw a type of pony quite new to her. She never forgot seeing it for the first time. Instead of the insignificant scrub ponies, which were all she had ever seen, it was stocky, more like the cobs of today, with hairy legs and big feet. It stood several inches taller than the little biscuit-coloured pony standing with it, indeed bigger than any pony she had ever seen. And instead of the usual dun, grey or brown colour, its coat appeared to be a striking blue.

Anarhys also did a double take when he saw the pony with Dara. Yrwen hadn't had time to tell what him how Dara had treated the little cow, and he had been too far away to see properly what he did, but he knew it was something odd. Dara himself seemed odd. The whole set-up seemed very peculiar. Now the Ancestors were left behind he felt he had entered an alien world of strange people, animals and Spirits, and he almost thought he might be living in one of those stories they told round the fires on winters' evenings back home, or in a weird dream. He glanced over towards the familiar mountains he had left behind, but the drizzling rain hid them from him, and they were no comfort.

"What do you think of our ponies?" Mabin asked him as they stood together.

"Different," said Anarhys guardedly.

"Do you like them?"

"Yes," said Anarhys after some thought.

"They are worth a good bronze axehead to us. Our houses need repair. Our Ancestors will like the glittering bronze and will help us."

"Yes, the blue pony must be especially valuable."

"Both ponies must reach the Gogarth Headland to be traded for bronze. The Gogarth People need stock animals. We need that axe. You do understand me, don't you Anarhys? Dara and Caersws must come back here safely with a good bronze axehead, and then you can take your cow home. Dara has treated it so it will be ready to travel home when you return. I know where your village is. If the deal is not kept I shall find you. I saved your life, Anarhys. Don't forget."

Anarhys thought of Iago, anxiously awaiting his return back at Gwrtheyrn, and wanting news of Yrwen. "I won't forget. We'll do whatever we have to and we'll get back as fast as we can. You'll get your axe."

"Thank you, Anarhys. And I don't need to warn you to watch the mountains for warnings of invaders, do I?"

Anarhys was silent. Not this again, he thought. First my father, then this man, turning myths and legends into real people. Even I'm starting to believe in them.

"Anarhys, you do know, don't you, about the Iron Men?" said Mabin.

"Mabin," said Anarhys slowly, "my father warned me about the Iron Men. We make up stories about them. We frighten the little children with them if they don't help us with the work. We imagine them to be giants, with swords made of metal ten times stronger than bronze, and ready to attack us savagely for no reason at all. But I don't believe they're real." He saw Mabin's face go still.

He was aware of movement about himself and Mabin,

as others prepared the livestock for the next leg of the journey. Caersws, the oldest of the group, and Cavan were ready with their back packs and staffs; the strange boy Dara, smaller and slighter than any of them, was standing with the ponies; Yrwen and the black dog stood fretting together with the remaining two cows, waiting to go. Anarhys realised that Mabin was standing very still and straight, and looking hard at him, as if they were the only two people that mattered at that moment. The older man, with his looks and bearing appeared suddenly impressive and consequential to him, and he took an involuntary step back.

"Watch the mountain summits when you can see them," Mabin repeated, his eyes piercing into those of the younger man. "Caersws and you must watch. If you see warning fires turn inland towards the mountain valleys. Do you understand me, Anarhys? The Iron Men are seagoing people. Turn inland if you see beacons."

"Yes I will, Mabin," said Anarhys, "I'll turn inland if there are any beacons on the mountain tops," and even as he said it he was thinking again that they could barely see the mountain tops most days because of the mists and rains. For a moment he wondered if the warnings of the Iron Men had something in them after all, but the idea seemed so preposterous that he pushed it consciously to the back of his mind.

"Times are hard for all of us," said Mabin. "We all have to make difficult decisions. Now, may the Spirits be with you all, and not against you." He waited for the group to leave.

Five people – Caersws, Anarhys, Cavan, Yrwen and Dara – set their backs towards him to travel northwards with their livestock towards their destination. On their right were the foothills of the mighty mountain, yr Wyddfa, a place so sacred that not even the greatest of the Ancestors were buried there. To their left was the sea.

Chapter Five

The expanded group travelled north, parallel to the coast, keeping the mountains to the right and the ocean to the left. The coastal plain was sparsely populated, but their way had become a path, sometimes passing between forlorn walls of small deserted fields. Later it would become a wet track. The few inhabited hamlets they passed were skirted quietly, but they were untroubled by the residents. The mist blew away, but the skies were as grey as ever.

Yrwen took the lead this time; with her was the diminutive figure of Dara, and hard on Dara's heels were his two ponies. Tramping behind him with the black hound Anarhys was puzzled as to why the two ponies kept their heads so close to the boy's shoulders. It was almost as though they were his friends and wouldn't be parted from him. At Gwrtheyrn they treated their ponies like cattle and herded them from behind, but Dara sometimes put his hand out and rubbed their necks, almost with an affection, the way Yrwen might do to her dog. It was interesting and different, and to his surprise Anarhys liked it. He and

Cavan walked as outriders a few feet to the left and right of the animals.

"Ready for a break?" shouted Caersws from the back, as the pale brightness of the sun behind its cloud covering tipped past the zenith. They had walked several hours and most of them were stiff and tired. The path was becoming marshy, and the air smelled of bog and peaty grass.

"Stream up ahead," Yrwen shouted back, as the sounds of running water came to her ears.

"Sounds like a good place to stop," Cavan called to her. "I want to wash my feet. They're so hot and tired.

"Not until the cows have drunk," said Yrwen, as they arrived at the stream and fanned out on the bank.

"And ponies," added Dara, but the animals needed no invitations. It had been a long morning for them too. They splashed into the cold running water, churning the muddy bottom, reviving their weary legs and drinking thirstily. Anarhys looked at the cows protectively from the bank. They were the assets he was responsible for. And so, it would seem, was Yrwen. He saw Cavan slip his pack from his shoulders.

"I'm going upstream to drink where the water's clear," Cavan said, and walked away. For some reason Yrwen followed him. Cavan stopped ahead of her and removed his leather cape and woollen top. When she caught up with him she realised why.

"Your shoulders are horribly raw from carrying the back bag," she said to him. She looked at the narrow red welts across the tops of his shoulders and over his collar bones in front where the straps had rubbed. They looked hot and painful.

"I know," he said, bending down by the chilly water and splashing some over his back.

Stepping nearer, Yrwen looked more closely. "Here, let me," she offered. "Kneel down, Cavan." He knelt gracefully and readily, and Yrwen cupped her hands into the stream letting the cooling water pour out over Cavan's shoulders. Anarhys, following behind, saw them together with misgivings, and saw straight away that this was not simply a friendly gesture. Yrwen was stroking Cavan's shoulders with some tenderness, breathing deeply and enjoying the masculine smell of his warm, damp skin, and the closeness of his body. Cavan, clearly enjoying the sensation, was in no hurry to stop her. Anarhys was worried. It wasn't part of Iago's plan for Yrwen to fall for Cavan, he thought, and if she does how will I ever be able to persuade her to take a husband and stay on Gogarth?

"It's not like you to nurse people," he said to her as he caught up with them.

"I was only helping Cavan cool his shoulders. Look at them, they're burning."

"I can see, but I'll do that, Yrwen," said Anarhys. "You go back and check the cows."

Cavan stood up. "That's better. Thanks Yrwen. Let's get a drink here where the water's clear," he said. And to Anarhys's consternation they took a drink together from the edge of the stream, their heads almost touching.

"We're going to wash our feet, aren't we, Cavan? They're hot and dirty," said Yrwen, sitting down to take off her worn leather boots. Yrwen was testing him, and again Anarhys felt his leadership tilting out of balance.

He saw Cavan hesitate, and waited to see what his friend would do,

"Perhaps we should go back to the cows," Cavan answered after a moment, to Anarhys's relief. We can clean our feet off later."

"All right Cavan," agreed Yrwen, but instead of walking down the bank with the other two she waded petulantly back along the stream to the cows, splashing up water as she went. Anarhys knew Cavan well enough to see his friend was watching her admiringly, and his heart sank. It was unusual for young people who had grown up together in a village to become attached, and the standard custom was for the girls to marry out of their tribes, but these two seemed to be more than just friends. He wondered whether it was recent, or whether his father had known about it. It would be reason enough for sending Yrwen away to find a husband.

Back at the cows, another setback. Anarhys found Caersws sitting on the bank with his feet in the stream and the others standing round him. Dara was kneeling beside him.

"He's done some serious damage to his ankle joint," he said. "It's bad. Look."

Anarhys looked at the older man's leg, and then at his face. When Caesws pulled his foot out of the water they could see the joint was swelling, almost as they watched. He put it back in the cold water with a grunt of relief. Under the weathering and smoke his face looked white.

"Stay there, Caersws, and I'll get some food," was Cavan's practical suggestion, and he opened his bag to share round the bread and fish Menith had packed. They were hungry enough to enjoy it, dry as it was. They took their waterproof capes off and sat on them in a close circle around Caersws.

"You'll have to go on without me," Caersws said to Anarhys. He wasn't eating much. "I'll go back. It hurts, but I can lean on my stick." He cast a glance at Dara as he did so.

"How did it happen?"

"The pony stood on me as it came up the bank. The big one."

"It's your own fault, Caersws, you shouldn't have been there. She couldn't help where she put her feet," said Dara, looking anxious.

"You shouldn't go back alone," Anarhys remonstrated. "Think of the dangers. Another accident. Wolves. Cold and wet. The threat of hungry men." For a moment Anarhys and Caersws looked into each other's eyes, then both glanced rapidly at the mountains. As expected, no lit beacons.

"I'll be all right. You don't have the time to come with me, and it won't take more than a day to go back. I've got my stick to lean on, and I'll take some food, and stop off at a hamlet if I have to. They'll know of Mabin and me so I should be safe."

"You could take a pony, Caersws," suggested Dara.

"And what would your father say if I brought a pony back with me when it's needed for trading? No Dara. You must take both ponies on to Gogarth and bring home a good bronze axe-head. You'll have to do it without me. The others will help. You will, won't you Anarhys?"

Anarhys thought of their hostage cow at Ddu village, and knew he was in no position to refuse to take Dara to

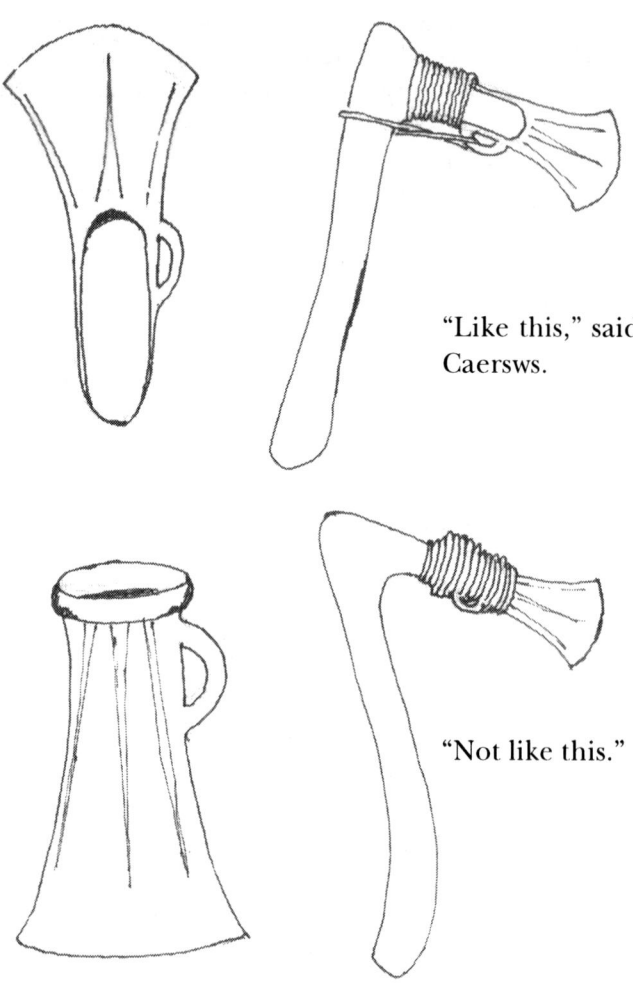

"Like this," said Caersws.

"Not like this."

Gogarth. He saw he was clearly distressed for Caersws. "But you were going to choose the axe-head, Caersws. I don't know much about bronze. How can I tell which one we need?" said the boy.

"Well Dara," said Caersws after a moment. "You need to hold it in your hands. If there is too much Cornish tin in the bronze it will feel brittle and could easily break, although that would be unlikely because tin is expensive and difficult to transport in these times. Too little tin and it will be soft, and won't sharpen properly, so feel the cutting edge; make sure it will stay sharp. The same if there's too much lead in the alloy: the copper mine on Gogarth Headland is so deep it's hard for them to get it out, so they may put in extra lead to make up the bulk and render it easier to cast, but the blade will be poor quality. Don't look at one that has a silvered surface. The silvering is just for looks, it'll be costly and you won't know what's under it. Make certain it attaches to the haft with a proper socket, and is wedged in tightly, either with pegs, rivets or ridges inside the hollow of the socket." He sketched out what he wanted to show Dara with his finger in the mud beside him. "Not like this, with an open attachment." He outlined another shape in the mud of the river bank. "Like this, with a socketed attachment. And there should be a loop on the axe head itself to attach it to the handle with a strip of leather. Try it out, and slice something with it so you get a feel of how it's weighted, and what the handle is like."

All eyes were on him. Every ear was listening hard. Far from wishing he didn't have to take Caersws' advice as he had earlier at Ddu Village, Anarhys was now wishing he could be doing business at the Gogarth Headland alongside them. "And our sickles?" he asked. "Have you any advice about them for us?"

"Harder rather than softer metal, the toughest you can see. They have to last for as long as possible without constant sharpening. They will need to be sharpened sometimes, of course, so make sure they are not too small and fine, or they'll wear away too quickly."

"Would you like to take our dog with you, Caersws?" Yrwen offered unexpectedly, concerned for him.

"You'll need him yourself, Yrwen, but thank you. It's Dara that's worrying me though. He is very young."

Anarhys expected Dara to reassure them all that he would be perfectly happy to go with them, but the boy looked from one face to the next, his own face fearful, clearly unhappy at what was happening. When Cavan tried to put his hand on his arm, Dara jumped back, then stepped over to the horses and stood close to them, taking comfort from them.

"Dara is unusual," said Caersws quietly to Anarhys, Yrwen and Cavan, echoing Mabin's earlier words. "When I have gone back he will stick closely to one of you. Whichever one it is, please, keep your eyes on him."

"We'll do our best, Caersws," Anarhys ventured. "But if you really are going back alone you need to get going, and we have to press on to Gogarth." He stood up. Wordlessly Caersws pulled his feet out of the cooling water and looked at his leg. He picked up his stick from behind him and stood up awkwardly, taking all his weight on one leg and his stick. Cavan held out his shoulder bag to him. Caersws took a little food out for himself and then handed it back. He took the hands of each of them to say Goodbye, and his hands felt hot and dry. He walked over to Dara and spoke to him for a few moments before turning south towards the sun, hidden as ever behind cloud cover, and set off back along the path they had just walked.

Anarhys watched gloomily as Caersws limped away from them lopsidedly, helping himself with his staff. Walking together quietly during the morning the two men had formed a tentative bond. Without Caersws his travelling companions now consisted of difficult Yrwen, strange Dara, and – well, Cavan was an ally, but there was the complication of whether he had fallen for Yrwen. Only the cattle, horses and dog were not causing any problems at present.

"Better move on," said Anarhys, and walked over to the ponies. "Ready to go, Dara?" he asked kindly.

"Yes, I suppose so." Dara was still watching Caersws' figure retreating. Yrwen picked up the back bag from the ground and put it on her shoulders. "Why isn't Cavan carrying that?" he added.

"Sore shoulders," said Yrwen shortly, pulling the bag onto her own back. "We'll all have a go at carrying it." Dara's question seemed a strange one to ask; there was no reason why Cavan should carry it all the time. It was going to be some time before she realised that Dara found any change in his life difficult, even a small one like the back bag being carried by different people.

Cavan took the lead, and set off with the two cows stepping dutifully behind him. They were tired now, and their heads hung as they walked. Cavan slowed his pace for them, but was aware that they needed to move on as quickly as possible. Dara walked after the cattle with the ponies' heads nodding at his shoulder, and Yrwen and Anarhys brought up the rear with the black dog.

"How much further, Anarhys?" Yrwen asked him.

"We cross the River Seiont later today, then the track climbs higher and there's a stretch of moorland where we camp just this side of Gogarth. Tomorrow morning we'll go up onto the Gogarth Headland to trade, and be on our way home by nightfall."

"I'll miss my cows when they're gone," mused Yrwen aloud.

And I could easily be missing you, thought Anarhys to himself, although in reality he couldn't imagine leaving Yrwen at Gogarth and returning home without her. Attempting to rid himself of the guilt of colluding in Iago's plan to marry her into another tribe, he said, "You never know, Yrwen, you might meet somebody up there that you really like, and will want to stay."

Yrwen laughed wryly. "Unlikely," she said. "I like Cavan, thanks."

The River Seiont entered the sea at the port of Caernarvon, but the route to Gogarth crossed it higher up. When Anarhys and his companions came to cross it they were faced with a stretch of brown, turbulent water, much wider than the one where Anarhys had his accident. Beavers had dammed it on its way down, slowing the flow, and in the past men had laid stones on the riverbed to make a broad, safe crossing point. Today the river was shoulder-high, and the crossing impossible to attempt on foot. The group stood together, each asking himself how it could possibly to negotiated, while the cows and ponies dropped their heads to crop the short marshy grass.

They were all tired. Anarhys' head ached with fatigue, his legs felt as though they would move no more. Dara's knees buckled as soon as they stopped, and he lay down full length near his ponies.

"There must be a way to cross," said Anarhys. "How do other travellers get over to Gogarth?"

"Boat perhaps?" suggested Cavan. "Might be a ferry man. How did you cross when you came with Iago?"

"There was a boat. That was years ago though. I can't remember whereabouts it was."

They looked around. They were still on the coastal plain, and the land was flat and sedgy. Stunted alder trees, covered in moss, grew along the river bank. In places where it widened reeds fringed both sides of the bank, rustling in the westerly wind breezing off the sea. No birds were singing, and there was a sense of abandonment. To the east, in the far distance, were the Great Mountains, among them the yr Wyddfa, taller and mightier than all the others. Their heads were hidden in cloud. They weren't the comforting mountains of home where their Ancestors lived: they had vanished out of sight some time ago. They had to manage without the help of the Ancestors.

Yrwen, for all her weariness, took the black dog down to the reeds, and pushed among them. To her surprise she saw they were growing on the ruins of an old beaver dam. She pushed her way further, floundering through the rotting roots and cutting her fingers on the sharp leaves, and there, hidden among the rushes, was – exactly as she had hoped – a boat. She let out a yell. Anarhys and Cavan, despite their exhaustion, came quickly, and gazed down at the boat lying in the reeds.

It was a simple river boat, flat bottomed, about twenty feet in length, built of alder planks and sewn together with willow strips. One of the planks was loose and needed repairing, but it might be made watertight. They looked at it, wondering who it belonged to.

The River Spirit of the Seiont was mighty and the water flowed past them in an everlasting roar as they surveyed the boat. The sound hid the footfalls of a man approaching. He stopped to look at the cows and horses with greedy interest, and at Dara asleep on the ground beside them. His legs were bowed, the result of rickets, making him stand shorter than most people, but he was stocky and muscular. He carried a short-distance bow in one hand, and stealthily fitted a flint-tipped arrow into it.

Cavan, standing with Anarhys and Yrwen by the boat, had a premonition that all was not right. He glanced over to check on Dara and the livestock, and was shocked to find he was looking along the shaft of an arrow levelled directly at him. He stopped absolutely still, too startled to move. The bowman took a step towards them, the arrow still at the ready. Anarhys and Yrwen, following Cavan's stare, realised what was happening, and went rigid. Dara was still stretched out on the ground asleep. There was menace in the air. None of them spoke. When the bowman did eventually articulate it was in a flat, guttural voice:

"Come out of the reeds," he commanded, with a chuck of his head, still aiming the arrow towards them. As the three stepped back onto the marshy grass Anarhys saw out of the corner of his eye that Cavan had caught hold of Yrwen's hand. "That's my boat. What are you doing with it? Do you want to cross the river?" he added, the arrow-head still pointing directly at them.

"Yes, we do," said Anarhys finding his voice. "Can you take us?"

"What have you got to pay for the passage over?"

Not much, thought Anarhys. A passage across the river was not worth a cow, and besides, they needed them to trade on the Gogarth Headland. In the back bag, as well as the food, there was a piece of ironstone for starting fires and a small fishing net. They all had knives, but these were necessary for their journey. He wasn't going to let his father's gold disc go for a mere boat trip, but somehow they had to get over the river to the other bank with the livestock. The boat was evidently used as a ferry, and might even be big enough to take the cattle and ponies.

The man's gruff voice had woken Dara, and he got to his feet, alarmed.

"It's all right, Dara," Anarhys said to him. "There's a ferry. It needs some timbers stitching, but it'll probably carry us all. The only thing is though, the ferryman needs payment."

"He can't have the dog," said Yrwen, glancing down at the hound growling in its throat by her legs.

Dara looked into her face with understanding. Losing your dog was a serious misfortune. Quietly he pulled up his tunic. It seemed an odd gesture to make, but then Anarhys saw what he was doing. Wound around Dara's waist and hips were lengths of leather, some quite wide, others very fine. He undid several of the finest strips and held them out to the bowman. They would be ideal for repairing the stitching on the boat. With relief, Anarhys watched the bow-legged man lower his bow, remove the arrow from it, then take the leather cords from Dara with a nod.

"Tomorrow I'll come back," he said. "You can help me," and so the deal was done. Then he added in the same gruff voice, "I have fish. If you let me have milk from that cow I'll give you some."

★★★

As night fell that evening four exhausted travellers sank down for sleep round a small sad fire to the sound of the river rushing past among the scents of charred fish and sweet, marshy grass. The black dog lay with its head on Yrwen's legs, until they cramped and she pushed him off. They had no idea at all whether the ferryman would return in the morning to take them across the river, whether the boat would hold them all, or whether, even after repair, the boat would reach the opposite riverbank safely.

For the second night Anarhys slept badly. He rose twice to put a piece of alder branch on the fire, and heard Cavan do the same. He recalled his home village of Gwrtheyrn, down by the sea. In a half-awake state he imagined himself climbing the mountain that soared over the settlement, clambering up a tiny path through the scree, then making his way awkwardly across the rocks to a circular grassy hollow, concealed from all eyes except the birds flying above him. There was a children's stone shelter, roofed with hide, and he saw himself as a young boy playing with friends there, and later on girls, happy to spend time with him.

Chapter Six

As he pulled himself to his feet at a grey sunrise next morning Anarhys massaged his arms and legs. His neck was stiff, his limbs were sore, and his head ached from lying awkwardly on the ground. He had been happy enough to lie down last night, but now he longed for the heathery beds and pillows of home. When the others scrambled to their feet their faces too looked lined and grey, and they rubbed their bodies roughly, as he had, so he knew they were feeling just as wretched. Cavan walked downriver to find a willow tree and brought back leaves for them to chew to ease their headaches. Only when they had breakfasted on the last of the bread and dried fish did they feel they could face the river crossing.

The ferryman had not yet turned up, so all they could do was wait, and hope he would come. They waited anxiously until mid-morning, then to Anarhys' relief, the same bow-legged man appeared, followed by another fellow, who spoke only occasionally, and then in the same gruff way. Anarhys and Cavan accompanied them to the reeds and helped pull the boat out and up the river where it could be moored to the bank to do the repairs.

Yrwen went to check the fire was out and spread the ashes. "Come and help me, Dara," she said, but the boy backed off.

"I don't like fire," he said simply. "You do it, Yrwen. I'll get the animals together," and he started over to where the ponies and cattle were grazing quietly.

"Don't like fire?" Yrwen called after him. "Why ever not?"

"Frightening."

"There'll be lots of fires at the foundry on Gogarth. Big ones, with belching smoke. What will you do then?"

Dara didn't answer. Yrwen was nonplussed, but she still had a headache and pushed the conversation out of her mind with a shrug then went to get on with her work. She and the black dog helped gather the livestock up and take them down to the reeds where the men were working on the boat. The ferryman looked at the animals.

"That blue pony's too big. You'll have to tie it to the stern and make it swim," he grunted, moving his gaze to the water rushing by them. "The small one will be all right, but it'll have to stand still in my boat."

"I'll make sure it will," Dara assured him. Anarhys wondered how, and waited to see what would happen. There didn't seem to be an easy way to get the livestock on board, but he thought the strange boy might be able to do something. The boat was pulled up tight to the bank, but the cows and pony would have to jump over the sides into it, and it was pitching and swinging in the water. While they waited for the men to complete the repairs Dara stood in front of the dun pony, holding his open hands on its shoulders, and Anarhys saw it relax, just as Yrwen's cow had relaxed when he had treated it two days earlier. Its breathing slowed, its head dipped to the ground, and its eyes half closed. By the time the riverboat was ready to board the dun pony looked half asleep, and it followed Dara submissively to the vessel, gave a tiny hop over the gunwale, and stood quietly on the flat floor of the vessel. The two cows scrambled in behind, taking comfort from its calmness. Anarhys was impressed. He helped Dara make a halter from the strips wrapped around himself, and tied the other pony to the stern of the boat.

With the extra weight of the load it was going to be difficult to push the boat into the river. Yrwen and the men strained against it until it slid off the mud and into the current, and scrambled on board before it was swept downstream. The blue pony was dragged off the bank after it. The boatmen reached quickly for oars, and started to row, and as the ferry was hurled downstream it started to make headway across the river to the opposite bank.

It was a turbulent, frightening crossing. Even with the weight of the animals acting as ballast, the live cargo was rocked as the River Spirit beat against the planks of the boat. The humans clung on as well as they could, and the animals stood with their feet spread, rooted to the base of the boat. Yrwen's black hound hunched by her feet. Dara sat rigid in the stern, never taking his eyes off the head of his pony as it dipped and tossed in the current behind them. The boat shipped water, soaking their feet. Through it all, the bow-legged oarsman and his mate, faces impassive, never ceased their rhythmic rowing. They were wholly professional, the great muscles in their arms never seeming to tire, a glance over their shoulders as they neared the opposite bank the only time their bodies worked out of a perfect tempo. Their passengers, despite their experiences of being on the waters at their own villages, were truly thankful to reach the opposite shore,

As the boat slowed at the far side of the river and slid its prow into the mud on the bank, the ferryman's mate climbed out and held it fast. Anarhys and Cavan followed, and held the gunwales tightly. The animals spilled out over the sides in a rush, and stood shaking, thankful for dry land under their feet again. The blue pony, exhausted but alive, was untied from the stern and shook herself hard, soaking them all.

Anarhys, Cavan, Yrwen and Dara stood on the bank of the River Seiont with their precious animals, watching the two ferrymen pull the boat back upriver, then start their return trip across the torrent of water. Anarhys had an overwhelming sense of gratitude that the Water Spirits had protected them all after all, and allowed them to come this far in their travels. He thought of how all their lives were permeated by the presence of water: the streams and rivers of their homeland, the sea filled with its natural larder by their villages and the rain pouring down on them much of the time. He knew the Spirit of this river needed be kept appeased, not only to thank it for their safe passage, but also to protect them during the crossing on their return journey. He was not to know that none of them would come back that way. Not even Cavan foresaw it.

"We must offer the River Spirit a gift," he decided. "What do we have between us?"

"Knives," said Cavan, reaching into his waistband for his. "We all have them. We'll make an offering of one. We can choose whose is worth the most, and give that to the Spirits."

"I have my bone needles for treating ailments. I could offer those as well. I don't really want to, though," Dara said, trying to be helpful and untying the leather bag of bone needles from his waist. "I should have treated Caersws with them before he went home," he added wistfully. I wish I had done. I never thought. It would have helped his knee. I hope he reached home safely."

"I didn't realise you could use your needles for humans as well as animals," Cavan said, taking out his own knife. On the handle, which was worn and polished, and as befitted the son of a priest, he had carved a delicate circled pattern. The flint blade was carefully curved.

"Yes, of course," said Dara dismissively, "I often help our villagers when they're sick or injured." He took his own knife from his belt. The others inspected it curiously, to see what it had to tell about its owner. It had been meticulously made, almost obsessively, thought Anarhys, and was an exquisite piece of work; a small blade, with a haft that had been made to fit perfectly into his hand.

"Not the needles, Dara," Anarhys decided, eliminating one object to make it easier, and thinking at the same time that they would be of no value to the River Spirit. Yrwen and Anarhys took out their own blades

They compared the knives before them. Yrwen's was plain, and narrow where it was sharpened daily, and had a carefully oiled handle. The knife in Anarhys' hand was appropriate for the son of the village Elder: its blade was not flint like the others, but cast in lustrous bronze. It was not too difficult to decide which knife should be offered to the River Spirit.

"It's yours, Anarhys," Yrwen pointed out. "It's bronze, magical. It's come from the earth and the River Spirit will want to take it back into the earth. We can't offer the Spirits a knife that's never been used, which we should, because we don't have one. Yours is the one They will want."

I suppose Yrwen's right, thought Anarhys. I'll have to manage without it for a bit, and maybe replace it at Gogarth. He studied the knife lying comfortably in his hand. Losing it was would be like losing an arm, a faithful friend even, but it had to be done to satisfy the Spirit here. He looked at the river, saw the ferrymen had almost reached the far bank, and with a silent prayer to his Ancestors so far away on the mountains, he put it across his knee, and forced the handle off, letting it fall uselessly to the ground. He looked reverently at the blade gleaming mysteriously in his hand, and knelt down by the river. He laid it on a flat stone, took another stone in his hand, and with an enormous awareness of his sacrifice, broke it in half. He picked up the two pieces, rose to his feet, and threw them, sending them out as far as he could across the rushing waters. They all watched silently as the two fragments soared through the air, vanishing from sight before they entered the river, and Anarhys imagined them being tossed and tumbled through the boiling water on their way back to the earth of the river bed.

Cavan, watching his friend make this sacrifice, remembered their village back home. Without warning he had a mental image in his head of Anarhys's father, Iago, climbing alone up the path on the mountain above, then turning off to clamber over the rocks to the grassy hiding place among the granite scree. It was the same patch of grass hidden among the rocks that Anarhys had been dreaming about early that morning. In his mind's eye he could see the ocean that lay between the beach of his settlement and the horizon, and to his surprise he could make out five black dots sailing on it. He shook his head, and the picture vanished, leaving him puzzled. His visions often revealed knowledge to him, but this one made no sense at all. Why on earth would Iago be making his way to a children's hideout? Forgetting the dots on the sea, he felt a sudden inexplicable need to protect Yrwen from something; he had no idea what, and he had to stop himself from hurrying over to be close to her.

Yrwen set off again at the front with Dara, the blue pony and the dun nodding their heads rhythmically by Dara's shoulder, then, lagging behind a little came the two tired cows. Cavan fell in with Anarhys at the back, the black dog at their feet. The track had become narrower and boggier as it started to climb towards the open moorland, and the going became more difficult. Leather boots became caked in wet mud, weighing down their feet and shortening their steps.

"When the knife went in the river, I saw your father, Anarhys," Cavan said to his friend as they walked on together at the back.

"Did you, Cavan? How did he look?" It was never a surprise when Cavan told Anarhys about his visions. They had grown up together and his insights had seemed quite normal to both of them. Often they were useful.

"I didn't see his face. When I saw him he was climbing the path up the mountain above the village. It looked as though he was heading for the hideout – you know, the one among the stones on the mountain. But I don't know what he was doing because the image vanished before he got up there."

Anarhys digested this, thinking of Iago's warning about lighted beacons. "Not to the summit? He wasn't going up to light a beacon?"

"I don't think so. He wasn't carrying any wood, and there's none on the top. I'm sure he was going to the hideout."

"We'll ask him when we get back," Anarhys said, smiling for a moment at the thought of being home, and as he did so saw that they had come out on to open moorland. The track broadened out, became less sticky to negotiate, and they found they could walk along the side of it on the wet grass. Height gave them a view of the sea: it appeared as grey and forbidding as ever, and was topped with white foam. They had a view of the mystical island of Mon, about a mile away across it. This was where Caersws had spent time learning the arts of bronze work. The strait between mainland and the island was fast and dangerous, full of rocks and currents, a natural protective barrier to anybody trying to cross to its holy shores. Nobody but the initiated landed on Mon. Anarhys shivered, looking at its ominous aspect.

For a while the travellers trekked parallel to its forbidding coastline, keeping their eyes forwards, watching out for a sight of Gogarth Headland. They paused at the next stream they came to and cleaned the mud from their boots and leggings as well as they could, while the animals rested and drank. The rain had held off but black clouds were banking up from the west, and they pushed on as soon as possible. A few minutes later Anarhys, walking as usual at the back, saw that Dara's tunic still had lumps of mud sticking to them. Being small, the ponies stepping behind him had splashed wet mud up his back as far as his neck. It was still clinging to him. Better send him back to the stream to get properly cleaned up, thought Anarhys.

"Hey Dara," he called forward to him, "you need to get more clay off your clothes than that. Why don't you go back to the stream and make a better job of it?"

Dara stopped. "If you say so, Anarhys," he said mechanically.

"Will the ponies go on without you? If you're quick we could go on slowly, and you could catch us up when you can. Or I'll wait back a bit for you."

Dara stepped behind the ponies, and put a hand on the blue pony's rump. "Go on," he simply said, and they both walked forward obediently behind Yrwen. He turned back towards the stream.

"You carry on without us," Anarhys said quietly to Cavan and Yrwen. "I'll wait here for him and catch you up. I don't expect he'll be long." The rest of the party moved on across the moorland. It was entirely different to the lowlands they had just left behind. There were a few solitary trees, but they were stunted and bent, misshapen by the wind, so it was possible to see right across the landscape. Peat had already formed and the ground was covered in short moorland grass and heather. In places black bogs lay either side of the track, ready to sink unwary travellers who strayed too far. Some of the peat had been cut out to feed fires, and where this had happened there were deep pools of brown water, ice cold and still. A few of the pools were enormous, as big as a medium-sized roundhouse.

Anarhys sat down to wait on a clump of springy heather to wait for Dara. He faced into the wind, watching the sea, and the heather sank slowly beneath his weight. He observed his surroundings carefully. Not long now, he thought, and he would be able to see the Gogarth Headland, stretching out into the sea, the shape of a colossal beetle. Rising from it would be smoke from the metal smelting works, and it would be full of people – wild Gogarth men certainly, but still people They had seen barely anybody except the taciturn boatmen for two days now, and he was looking forward to mixing with other human beings again, seeing new faces, conversing with them, trading with them.

Remembering he was sitting there to wait for Dara, he turned his head to see how the boy was getting on at the stream. He was taken aback to see Dara had taken off his tunic and leggings in an attempt to clean them, and was standing with his back to Anarhys. When he turned round, Anarhys' felt his heart stood still. He almost fell off his heather bush with shock. He realized suddenly that Dara was not a boy at all. He was a girl!

Dara was a girl! Not a boy, but a girl. It explained why Mabin had been so careful about letting her go with them; it explained why Caersws had been reluctant to leave her with them when he had to turn for home; it could explain why Dara always sought out Yrwen's company and not his own, or Cavan's.

Anarhys tried to turn his eyes away, but couldn't. He was frozen in time. Suddenly he wanted to touch the sensitive skin on Dara's shoulders, run his hands along her thighs, feel her breasts beneath his fingers. She had become instantly desirable, and he could not imagine he hadn't realized that under those baggy clothes was a female figure. He kept his head down, watching her dress herself, as she turned from an enchanting picture of a young, semi-naked woman back to a human form clothed in shapeless brown garments. She was wrapping her leather strips back around her waist before Anarhys could bear to break his gaze. He stood up in the heather, facing away from Dara, but he could feel his heart picking up speed, and when she came up to him he could barely stop himself reaching out to her. All he wanted to do by then was to kiss her gently on her forehead, then not so gently on her mouth.

As Anarhys and Dara walked on quickly together to catch up with Cavan Anarhys felt his thoughts tumbling together. Should he tell Dara he had seen her dressing? Should he say – I know your secret, Dara? Or – I know you're a girl? Or even – would you like to lie down in the heather with me? Should the others know? He had no idea. There was a feeling of guilt that Mabin and Caersws had given responsibility of this girl to him – yet here he was wanting her for himself. As Dara took the lead again with Yrwen he said nothing, but found that all the plans and decisions he had been making for the expedition were melting away, and his head was filled instead with the image of Dara dressing herself by the stream.

At the front of the party Yrwen and Dara were walking together again. Coming along behind Anarhys could see that they had removed their stiff waterproof caps, and pushed them into their belts so that the sharp breeze coming in from the black clouds over the sea was blowing their hair round their heads, his sister's hair fine and fair, contrasting with Dara's coppery tresses. For the first time he watched the way they walked. Yrwen was clearly tired from their journey, but she walked with a confident stride, head up and shoulders squared, as though she was sunning herself in Cavan's admiring gaze. Beside her Dara, having no idea of Anarhys' appreciation of her, showed her weariness in the droop of her shoulders, her arms hanging heavily by her side, no longer bothering to rub her ponies' necks.

★★★

The five ships sailed through the roaring seas, past the western tip of the island of Britain, and then northward. They were sea-going vessels, deep-keeled, clinker-built, held together with iron nails as thick as man's finger, and carrying rawhide sails. A slanting, angry eye was painted in cobalt blue and black on either side of each prow.

Most of the crew were long-boned men, taller than Anarhys' race, with long dark hair plaited down their shoulders. Their tunics and leggings, saturated in sea water, had been woven on giant looms in coloured dyed wool many years ago, but the magentas, golds and sapphire blues were still visible. They were Celts – a European nation, who were learning about working the new metal, iron, and they too were enduring the savage weather and famine covering all of Europe and parts of Asia. Shortages bred disease, war and death. The hungry Celtic tribes, never shy of fighting, warred with other tribes and then among themselves. In desperation, some of the men, abandoning wives and children, left their countries to search for new lands which might support them. They did not go searching in peace.

The commander of the flotilla, Grey Wolf, had earned his position by being mentally and physically more powerful than his peers. His orders were given incisively, and obeyed implicitly by his sailors. Standing in the stern of the leading boat, a symbolic bronze torque of status on his neck, he eyed the Welsh coast hungrily for resources which he could harvest for himself – be they land, food or mineral wealth. He would take anything and everything he wanted, and by force if he had to.

Chapter seven

The breeze sharpened as they climbed across the moors and the shadowy cloud dropped its burden of rain, a little at first, then in sheets. They were thankful for waterproof capes and hats, but the ponies and cattle mooched dejectedly forward, heads lowered and tails clamped tightly down against the storm. The black hound, soaked already by its journey across the river, dripped along behind Yrwen. There was no protection from the elements across the barren landscape: trees that once grew plentifully across the countryside had been felled long ago by the bronzesmiths on the Gogarth Headland to fire their furnaces, and the wind blew straight across the land from the sea. Progress became, if anything, even more difficult.

Anarhys' ardour was cooled by the torrent of rain, but he was still shocked and intrigued by Dara. He guessed Mabin had sent her on her journey disguised as a boy for her own protection, but he wondered to himself whether there might be something more to it than that. He walked close to her two ponies, trying to find in them clues to the mystery. The dun pony, a castrated male, was nothing out of the ordinary – a plain, tough creature which would carry flesh through the winter, and live to see the spring on short rations. The blue pony, a mare, was something very different, and evidently the one Dara was especially attached to. She not only stood taller, but was prettier, with a kind face, big eyes, and sensitive muzzle. He saw that her short summer coat gave the appearance of being blue because she had a mixture of black and white hairs growing closely together. There was no white on her legs, mane and tail and they were as black and as shining as jet. She might be too tall to survive easily through the winter in these hard times for most people, but her unusual size and colouring would make her an attractive status symbol for a man who had the means to keep her. Anarhys thought of the Gogarth people; they would make enough money from their bronze trading to be able to afford to own a creature like this.

"Your big pony is a handsome creature," he said to Dara through the rain, as their faces and clothes dripped with moisture.

"Yes, she is," came the answer.

"I've never seen a pony with a blue coat like that before. Did you breed her?"

"Oh yes, we did. We had a good stallion which Caersws brought from Mon, and a big old mare which had a few white hairs in her coat. She's seen four winters now, but we might not be able to feed her through another one. She gets so thin. Father says there isn't enough food for all the livestock so she has to go." Dara, walking in front, was having to turn her head to answer Anarhys, and he looked appraisingly at her profile as she did so.

He thought that even the rain running down her face, and dripping off her chin could not spoil her delightful face, and wondered how he could ever have imagined she was a young man. "She has a name, too," Dara added.

"A name?" Anarhys thought he might be gaining this strange girl's trust, and was anxious to keep the conversation going.

"Blue. I call her Blue."

"Good name. Does the other pony have a name?"

"Oh no," said Dara dismissively. "The other one's just a pony. Blue's special." Then she turned to Yrwen. "What do you call your dog?"

"Well, he doesn't have a name," Yrwen answered, surprised. "I just call him Black Dog."

"He's faithful to you, Yrwen," said Dara. "You could call him Faithful."

"Yes, I suppose I could," Yrwen said thoughtfully. She glanced back at the black hound. There had always been dogs around the villages. Dogs and humans had developed together. They were inseparable. Dogs helped with the farming stock, warned the villagers of wolves, wild boar and other dangers, and played with the children. In return they were given food and protection. It was impossible to imagine settlements without their companionship and input. Her dog deserved a name.

"Faithful, then," agreed Yrwen, slightly unwillingly.

★★★

Heads down against the stinging rain which assailed them resolutely from the sea, the group did not see the sacred Stone Circle until they were almost upon it. The Stones loomed over them, each one almost twice a normal human height, set in an oval about thirty strides across its narrowest diameter. A quantity of white quartz pieces, the size of small stones, lay scattered on the wet ground within the Circle. They glistened in the rain, but Cavan knew they demanded the brightness of sunshine to discharge sparkle to their full potential. The group stood in silent awe and reverence, regarding the Stone Circle as it stood stark and brooding on the desolate hillside, a tribute to the unknown builders of the past. The Ancestors of many different tribes were here. From the start of history They had congregated at the many Circles that humans had erected for them across the countryside.

"We mustn't go inside," said Cavan at length. "We might disturb the Ancestors. Only the priests are allowed to enter."

"Why were the Stones assembled in a circle?" asked Dara in the quietness that followed.

"To confer with the Spirits," said Cavan. "In the days when we could see the sky, before it was always covered in cloud as it is now, the priests came here during the different seasons of the year and lined up the Stones with the heavenly bodies, so they could talk to the Ancestors. They used the sun, the moon, even the patterns of the stars. In that way the Ancestors would reply, telling them when the summer was ending so they could reap their corn. They could tell them when the sun would come back to start the growing season and when the days would start to lengthen in the winter. The Ancestors advised them when to collect their cattle and ponies from the hills, and house them in sheds, and when to let them out again in the spring."

"Not much sun now," grumbled Yrwen, as she shivered in the rain.

"No," agreed Cavan. "The Spirits haven't spoken to anybody properly during these last terrible years when we've hardly ever seen the sun. We can still talk to the Ancestors, but without the sun they can't speak to us and advise us about the farming year. All the priests who worked in the Stone Circles have gone."

"Cavan's father was a priest," Anarhys explained to Dara. "That's how he knows about it."

"It's true," said Cavan. "I remember when I was small my father used to leave the village in order to travel here for meetings with other priests, and hear what the Ancestors had to say. Then he'd come home to advise us what work was next to do on the farm. People always live by rivers and streams because neither we nor our livestock can live without fresh water for drinking, so the Stone Circles were built away from running water, high in isolated places like this. Then the priests could work with nobody to disturb them. They were highly educated people, and they needed the peace and silence to concentrate on their work."

"The Stones are massive. I never could work how they were transported from the mountains," Yrwen said, with a grudging admiration.

The Stones had been set up in the landscape over a millennium ago – and Cavan knew the mystery of how it had been done. He would have liked to show off to Yrwen – and Anarhys and Dara for that matter – and tell them exactly how the massive Stones had been raised from the mountains, brought through the landscape, and slotted upright into their present positions on the moors, but it was impossible. The ancient knowledge was not his to tell. Instead, he pointed out the tracks leading to the Circle that the priests had used to walk along to their gathering. "The paths come from every direction. We'll probably meet other people now who're using them to get to Gogarth to trade," he said.

Coming along the path leading from the Gogarth Headland there were indeed three figures. In the relentless rain the other group looked as wet and weary as themselves. They skirted the Stone Circle, and paused to speak when they reached Anarhys. Water dripped off their faces and capes, and they squelched along the soaking path, their tunics and leggings hanging on them heavily, full of moisture.

Anarhys greeted them. "This weather never seems to improve," he remarked to them in greeting.

The first man nodded, blowing rainwater from his nose as he did so. "Awful," he agreed. "I can't believe it will ever end. We've just come from the Gogarth Headland to trade, and it's just as bad there. Is that where you're heading with your livestock?"

"We are," said Anarhys. "How's business going up there?"

The man pushed his soaking hair off his forehead, and Anarhys saw that although he wasn't old, his face was grey and lined with worry and fatigue, just as his father's always was. "Fortunately for us it's better for those of us wanting to buy bronze than selling it. The Gogarth people are still mining and working metal, but with fewer people on the land they don't have the trade. They make more stuff than they can sell. You should do well. Look at this." He took off his back bag and opened it. Anarhys peered inside. Then he glanced sharply at the man's face.

"Arrowheads!" he exclaimed shortly, his heart giving a sharp thud. He was suddenly wary of this man. "Why arrowheads? Who are you going to fight with?" Cavan and Yrwen stepped up behind him and looked over his shoulder into the bag. Twelve bronze arrowheads lay heavily together in the bottom of the bag, the newly-cast bronze shining alive and golden. They were narrow and straight sided, with sockets and small barbs, not much more than an inch long, and beautifully finished. The edges were brilliant, freshly honed. They nestled together in a curiously threatening way, awaiting the fitting of their shafts.

"I hope I'm not going to fight with anybody at all," came the answer. "They're for defence. Our village stands at the base of a mountain, so if we were attacked we could climb up and shoot down on whoever it was. Because they're made of bronze the Spirits will fly with them. They'll find their mark."

"Who would attack you?" Yrwen asked quietly.

"Haven't you heard? Rumour has it the Iron Men are sailing up the Welsh coast looking for land. You should be watching the tops of the mountains for warning beacons, and be ready for them if they come."

The Iron Men again. They seemed to be on everybody's mind. Both parties glanced involuntarily at the mountains to the south, but their peaks were, as ever, veiled in mist.

"We did hear," said Anarhys. "But we don't honestly believe it. Surely it can't be true! Stories of the Iron Men are just that – stories to entertain one another round the fires in the evening, or to scare the children."

"I don't know," said the man, with the emphasis on the "I" and a shrug of his shoulders. "But we all need to be ready, just in case. The Iron Men are supposed to be cruel and terrible people, not a peaceful race like us. Be careful." A pause, then, "We must go on, we have to get back home. Have good trading on Gogarth. Make sure they give you hot food as part of the deal. You look as though you need it."

"Thank you, we will," replied Anarhys, Cavan and Yrwen. The Gwrtheyrn travellers watched the three figures move away from them with a pang of loneliness. The heavy rains formed an opaque curtain around them, and they looked around for other signs of human life. They had passed two fire pits used for cooking by the side of the track, but they had been quite cold and nobody had lit fires in them for a long time. The land felt emptier than ever. Unreservedly, feeling Yrwen close by him, Cavan put his arm around her shoulders. She looked as though she enjoyed his being there, accepting the warmth and strength from his body, and not pushing him away as he would have expected her to. With an infinitesimal feeling of being excluded, Anarhys thought of Dara, and looked eagerly behind him. She had stopped, and was standing by her ponies' heads. He went over to her.

"What are you doing, Dara?" he asked, kindly. She had taken some hide strips from around her waist, and was fashioning a halter on the blue pony's head. A length of leather hung down from the halter, and she picked up the end.

"I'm too tired to walk any more," she answered. "I'm

going to sit on Blue's back. It's all right, she won't need guiding. She knows to follow Yrwen, and I'll have this." She held the length of leather attached to the pony's halter in one hand. Anarhys watched her in surprise. She took three steps backwards, paused for a second, then vaulted so she was lying over the blue pony's wet back. A moment later she had wriggled a leg over, and straightened up so she was sitting astride Blue facing her ears. She leaned down for a second, and patted her pony's soaking neck. Through it all Blue had stood immobile, not even twitching an ear, evidently trusting her rider unreservedly. Sitting erect on the pony with her head above everybody else's, Dara took on a stately aspect. Her grey-green eyes shone down on them, her russet hair was darkened by the rain, and she had a small smile on her face. "Let's go, Yrwen," she said.

Yrwen was annoyed. Cold, wet and uncomfortable, she felt she too would like to be up on a pony, releasing the weight from her legs, feeling the warmth of its body through hers, and taking things easy herself. As children at Gwrtheyrn they had played with the ponies, and sometimes sat on their bony backs. She wished she hadn't capitulated quite so quickly to Dara's idea of naming her dog. She didn't like Dara looking down on her instead of up to her as he had done before, because he was shorter. She was somewhat taken aback to see Anarhys looking up in an admiring way.

Cavan saw her mutinous face, and understood what she was thinking straight away. "We'll stop in a while to rest," he said to her. "Maybe the rain will give us a break. Look, I'll walk with you, Yrwen," and he walked on to the track. "Do you remember riding the ponies at home? Before the rains the cattle and ponies went right up to the tops of the mountains, and sometimes we used to ride them back to the village."

"I don't remember that far back; it was too long ago."

"Oh yes, I suppose it must have been," Cavan went on, walking beside her in a companionable way in an attempt to take her mind off Dara. "But even in the rains we did. You must remember, Yrwen. Their backbones stuck into us and made us sore, and we didn't always stay on for long before we fell off. The ponies either shied or tripped, or wouldn't go in the direction we wanted them to. It saved our legs, mind, up on the mountains. Do you remember looking down on the village? We'd be up there, supposed to be looking after the livestock, and forget what we were doing because we were playing hide and seek among the heather."

"Yes, I do remember that," said Yrwen, trying do damp down her resentful feelings, and finding herself liking it when Cavan said her name. "And I remember one day when you hid so well, Cavan, that we never found you, and we had to come down without you. We got into terrible trouble with your mother. Your father was away on priest's business, and she was terribly worried. They sent a search party up onto the mountain with the dogs, and couldn't find you. When it was dark they came down and found you asleep in a corner of your roundhouse." She gave a very small giggle at the memory.

There was silence between them. Then Yrwen said, "I'm glad you're here, Cavan. It's horrible travelling like this, with the awful weather and not much to eat."

Cavan gave her arm a little squeeze. "Same here," he replied. He looked around. The torrent of rain was easing, and the visibility improving so they could see ahead and he looked hopefully for some shelter where they could pause for a rest. There were some whin bushes up ahead. The bushes weren't very tall but they would shelter them from the wind and rain if they kept low to the ground. The livestock would simply have to turn their tails into the rain. He led the way round them out of the worst of the wind, and stopped.

"This all right for a midday stop?" he asked Anarhys.

Anarhys said, "Good idea." His eyes scanned the landscape for a source of food. "Those look like bulrushes over there. Must be a pond. I'll get some roots. There isn't time to light a fire, we'll just have to eat them raw. I'll take the bag, but would somebody lend me a knife please?" Yrwen handed him the back bag; by now it was almost empty.

"There's not much grass," she pointed out. "The ponies will be all right eating short grass like this but the cattle need it longer for grazing."

"I know," said Anarhys quickly. "We won't stay long. We'll be down off the moor tonight where the grazing will be better. Take a bit off the cow, Yrwen. We must keep her milking, and the more we milk her the more she'll give." Yrwen took her cap off to use as a container again. The rain had seeped through the leather already, and her hair was wet. The cow was feeling as out of sorts as she was and tried to kick when she was milked. Yrwen took no notice and carried on while Cavan leaned down and held her cap under the udder.

Dara slipped off her pony. "I'll help with the bulrushes," she offered, taking out her knife. Feeling better after the break from walking, she glanced up at

Anarhys, her wet face framed with gleaming hair, her green-grey eyes bright. He felt a sense of pride as he walked tall beside her to a little black pond fringed with bulrushes. They worked together companionably for a few minutes, Anarhys pulling the plants out by the tall stems, Dara cutting them with her small sharp knife and putting the roots into the bag. The could smell the peatiness of the water, the greenness of the plants, the sodden earth of the bank.

"We'll cut plenty, then we'll have some for tonight too," suggested Anarhys, as the bag filled up. "But we need to leave enough for other travellers." They finished the job and stood up. Anarhys caught his breath as he cast his eye around. The rain had almost ceased and the view had opened up.

"Look, you can see other people on the moor," Dara exclaimed.

"Yes you can," agreed Anarhys. "They look as though they're walking on the paths." And it's good to see them, he thought, a sign of human habitation. With luck we might be getting close to Gogarth.

"We can see the sea," said Dara in wonder, and indeed they could. And not only the sea. Stretching out into it from the mainland, was a peninsular of land, higher and wider at the far end, where it was about a mile across. The sea washed its cliffs on all sides, and billowing from the side of an elevated central point was a mass of dark smoke. Anarhys and Dara observed it in silence until Dara spoke.

"Is that the Gogarth's Headland?" she asked.

Chapter Eight

Commander Grey Wolf looked into the leaden void of the sky above him, but the sun was hidden. He could see where it was in the sky behind the cloud cover by a faint brightening high in the west, and with the distant Welsh coast visible on his east side he could still navigate. At night though, with no stars visible to show him the way, he would need to anchor before dusk. However, Midsummer's Day had just passed, and there was plenty of daylight to continue sailing northward for a while. He decided that he might as well steer closer to landfall to see whether there was anything of interest there.

The turbulent sea was not an enemy to Grey Wolf, but his natural element. Although his ancestors had originated in northern Europe, his entire life had been spent on the west coast of Brittany, and he felt as relaxed and powerful in a boat on the Atlantic Ocean as he did on land. He watched with detachment the coiling swell, topped with pitching white horses. He tasted the salt on his lips and tongue, felt the rolling of his craft as it rode the waves. The roar of the sea, the mewing of gulls, the noise of the billowing leather sails and the rain beating on them, were more familiar to him than the sound of his own footsteps.

Finally he looked at his vessel with pride. It had been constructed by the best boat builders in Brittany, and he had overseen it from its beginning. They had used the strongest oak and the toughest leather; the nails holding it together had been forged by the best ironsmiths he could find. The men who sailed it under him were his family and comrades. One of them might attempt to take command from him, but only if he showed signs of weakness, and he was not going to let that happen. There were no slaves on board: slaves needed to be shackled or they could cause trouble, and a shackled slave was a liability on a ship. The place for them was on land, although if he took captives whilst ransacking the coastal villages he would take them on the ships with him to work in the mines they were searching for. Or they could trade or sell them back in Brittany. That was another way to accumulate wealth.

There were four sailors on board with him, and Grey Wolf looked at them speculatively. They were tired, wet and hungry, but would never admit to it. His first mate was the oldest man on the expedition, and even he was more likely to organise a mutiny than show a weakness.

"Head for the coast, Ronan," ordered Grey Wolf abruptly.

"Aye, Grey Wolf," replied his second-in-command. He showed no sign of relief, but gave the order to reset the sails. As the boat went about Grey Wolf glanced back at the rest of the flotilla to ascertain they had turned with him. There were four of them. He gave a grunt of satisfaction to see them manoeuvre round behind him. The vigorous south-west wind which had chased them up the Welsh coat now caught them broadsides, rolling the ship. Ignoring the change of movement, he turned his eyes to the coast.

The commander of the flotilla was intelligent and enterprising. He had no patience with the spiritual significance of metals, but for purely secular reasons had taken an enormous part in the trade of copper and bronze which brought about stability and wealth to sectors of his country's society. Through his acumen he had become part of the new upper classes, and had owned land, cattle, bronze ornaments and slaves. The impressive bronze torque on his neck shouted his status to anybody who saw him. When the colder, wetter weather came to Europe he had seen the economic bubble burst, and bronze had lost much of its value. Nobody wanted it any more. Some people even buried caches of it in the hope it would regain its worth in the future, and the quality of it deteriorated until eventually it even lost its spiritual significance. Grey Wolf looked quickly for new opportunities. Iron had been discovered and worked, and he knew in his bones that it would be the next great successful invention. Iron was what he was searching for, and in the expectation of finding it he had taken two men on his expedition to Wales who had the arcane knowledge of metalworking. Like any businessman, however, he was also on the lookout for anything that he could trade which would secure him profits.

Grey Wolf's eyes scanned the coastline as it emerged from the driving rain. He was searching for a village close to the sea, built by a stream or river. Here would be a landing place, fresh water, livestock, food, and potential slaves which he and his men could take for themselves. The job would be better done under the cover of darkness, when they could take the villagers by surprise, but for now he could mark his target, land elsewhere and then make camp until nightfall.

Three mountain peaks forked on the skyline, and through the spray he could see a rounded hill behind their shoulders, topped by a massive edifice which gave the hill the appearance of a woman's breast. He smiled to himself at the thought of women. He and his men had been at sea for a long time. He could see that the foot of one of the mountains slid right down into the sea, and at the bottom of its slope was the very sort of place he had in mind; he could just see the roundhouses of a village, half hidden in the valley, and he was aware that the movement about them must be people and livestock. He guessed there would be cattle there, the great status symbols and givers of life. His men were hungry and they would enjoy a feast.

For now, though, they must hide behind the curtain of rain, and make landfall further up the coast.

★★★

Anarhys looked at Dara and longed to take her hand. Instead he said, "It's the Gogarth Headland all right. Let's get back to the others. Grab the bag Dara, we've got food enough there," and they hurried back to the whin bushes. Yrwen was standing by the milk cow, one arm over its back, looking towards the sea and holding a cap full of milk. "Have you seen that piece of land in the sea? Is it the Gogarth Headland?" she asked, her voice brittle.

Anarhys grunted an affirmative. There was nervous excitement in the air between the four of them, and for once they felt they wanted talk. They crouched in the whins, out of the wind, sharing the food out between them.

"Now we're almost there, we need a plan of what we're going to do," said Anarhys, driving himself to become leader again. He felt young and inadequate in the face of his responsibilities at Gogarth but he was determined not to show it. "We'll be off the moor long before the sun starts its journey down the sky, and tonight we can camp by the stream in the valley where there's shelter. We'll have time to fish and cook, and get some rest before we start our business with the bronze makers tomorrow."

"And the livestock needs to rest too," Yrwen reminded them all. "Look at them. They're all tucked up behind."

"They are, but they're fitter than when they set out," Cavan pointed out. "A long breather on better grass should relax them. They'll have time to lie down and the cattle can cud. We can check their feet for soreness, and they can stand in the stream to cool their legs. They'll look great by the time we come to trade them tomorrow."

Yrwen was reassured, but she was anxious at the thought of leaving her beloved cows in the hands of other people, and especially with the Gogarth people with their wild reputation. She loved the cattle fiercely and protectively. "Hope whoever buys them looks after them as well as I do," she muttered.

"Don't worry Yrwen, they will," said Cavan. He pronounced her name as though he enjoyed saying it. "Cattle are too valuable, they are the Preservers of Life.

They give their milk freely to us and to their calves, they help to keep us warm in the winter, their hides clothe us, they provide fertilizer for our fields, they breed new life easily, and at the end of their lives their bodies become our food. But you know all this. Nobody is going to treat them with anything but respect, not even the Gogarth people. The Spirits wouldn't allow it without retribution."

"I hope you're right," said Yrwen.

Anarhys was thinking to himself – it will be impossible to do anything about finding a husband for Yrwen at Gogarth. I suppose we might make it part of a deal. Even if we met somebody she likes, where would we stay long enough for her get to know them? Anyway, I don't think Cavan would come back without her. We can still see the Gogarth Headland from up here, but it doesn't look friendly, even from here, and it's not a place I want to stay long. I'd really like to get back to Gwrtheyrn quickly.

"How much longer before we come down off the moor?" asked Dara, interrupting his thoughts.

Cavan and Anarhys both thought back to the time they had been here before, years ago. "I think I remember that there's a single standing Stone," Cavan said eventually. "Then there's a cairn of stones covering the grave of one of the Great Ancestors, but I don't think we'll see it. It's off the track, and we haven't time to look for it. Further on is the stream where we'll camp." He went on, "In my father's time all of this moorland was sacred land. You can still hear Ancestors talking to you if you listen." They listened. A few gulls, well fed on the thriving fishing stocks, mewed over towards the sea, the rain plipped off the sweet-smelling whin bushes, but only Cavan, listening out beyond these sounds, could hear the Ancestors whispering among themselves. He glanced over at Yrwen, and suddenly felt again that she needed protection. He didn't know why, because she was always so self-sufficient, and he didn't know what he should be saving her from, but he had a very strong sense that he wanted to shield her. He wondered if he had picked something out from among the murmurings of the Ancestors.

"There's nothing for them to eat here," she observed, only half-listening to Cavan, and concentrating instead on her cows. "The grass is too short. It's all right for your ponies Dara, they can nibble away on it, but my cows need longer grass. Can we get on now, and find something better for them to eat?"

Anarhys stood up. Cavan picked up the back bag with the precious bulrush roots in it. If they could get a fire going at their next stop they would be able to roast them. He put it over his shoulder, and winced as the straps caught where they had rubbed.

"Give it to me," Dara said. "Look, Blue can carry it, and I'll walk." Deftly she unknotted her makeshift halter and rein, and fitted them as a neckstrap and a loose girth around Blue's neck and body. Taking the back bag from Cavan, she attached it to them so it was hanging high up between the blue pony's legs, swinging a little, but out of the way of her knees, and loosely secure. "We'll have to take it off if we go through deep mud or water, or it'll get wet," she added, as the group set off yet again. The others watched; Cavan curious and Yrwen mildly amused. Anarhys was impressed. The rain stayed away as his party moved on towards the last camp before their trading destination. The Gogarth Headland was ahead on their left, and the mist-cloaked mountains on their right. As they walked the view changed slowly, but the ocean remained as grey and menacing as ever, topped with tossing white horses. Blue walked with her head by Dara's shoulder, the dun pony following behind.

"Blue should be all right too, shouldn't she?" Dara remarked to nobody in particular, thinking back to Yrwen's conversation with Cavan about how animals were treated. "A pony that you can ride's a status symbol too so she'll be treated with deference too, won't she?"

"She will," Cavan assured her. They didn't mention the dun pony. "They'll treat her like a treasure. She's amazing, Dara. How did you train her to let you ride her like that?"

"Oh she's very clever and I've always handled her since she was a foal, so it was easy," answered Dara. "As soon as she had lived through three winters I lay across her back and she never minded. When I first sat up on her I kept my head right down so as not to frighten her."

"What about guiding her?" asked Yrwen sceptically.

"I do it with my weight. If I sit to the left she steps left to balance us. Same to the right. I sit back and she slows, and I lean forward and she goes. I know some people put metal bars in their mouths to guide them, but I don't need to. I guess if I was riding in a battle a metal bar in her mouth would make it easier to stop or turn her quickly if she wasn't concentrating. But I wouldn't do it. She wouldn't like it. And anyway, I don't want to."

"No, I can see why not," Anarhys said quickly, and at Dara's mention of a battle gave an involuntary glance at the mountains. Nothing, to see, of course. He asked himself whether they would actually be able to see the flames of a fire through the wreathing mists that hung round the mountains, and squinted his eyes. Still nothing. He thought that if by chance the Iron Men existed, and that they were coming, Cavan would surely know through his second sight. He didn't realise that Cavan, for his part, was so certain in his own mind that stories of the Iron Men had been fabricated, that he never opened his mind to them.

They started to meet small groups of people walking on the moor. Later, as the path descended, they passed a single standing Stone, just as Cavan had said. Erect by the track it stood out of the Earth, shorter and narrower than a man, its edges sharp as though they had been chiselled. It appeared as a solitary feature of the landscape, quite unlike the Stone Circles with their clearly significant architecture. Yrwen, who hadn't seen one before, asked Cavan about it.

"They were erected by tribes who were here long before our people came, and long before our priests built the Stone Circles, They were markers for ways and directions, but we don't know exactly how they were used: the knowledge of those old nations was lost before we came. But what I can tell you is this: if you go and stand by one you'll feel an energy. The energy may once have been so strong that they could harness it and use it to their advantage, but we don't know how, or why. I wish we did."

Hearing this, Dara stopped by the standing Stone. She reached out, laying the palm of her hand against its cool, wet surface and closing her eyes to concentrate on her other senses. She thought she could hear the Stone singing tunelessly. It gave out a strength that she was certain she could tap into, if only she knew how. She looked back towards the Stone Circle they had passed. She could just make it out on the skyline, and was aware of a connection between the stone she touched and the Circle. More than that she could not work out, but she looked thoughtful as she walked away.

The wind eased as the group left the elevated moorland, and descended into the valley where the stream ran. Familiar now with crossing running water, the livestock plunged through it. Yrwen followed, carrying the back bag high over the surface with one hand, and holding a cow's tail with the other. Cavan grasped the black hound strongly, Dara held Blue's tail, and Anarhys held Dara's elbow. He hoped it looked as though he was helping her, but in reality he enjoyed the feel of her warm arm under his fingers. She didn't object.

"This looks like a camp site," Cavan pointed out as they reached the other side. "Look, there's a fireplace. Lots of travellers must have stayed here before."

"That overhanging bank will give us some protection," added Anarhys. "It's a good place to stop. Somebody's left dried peat from the moor, and sticks. We can use it as fuel for a fire, and we'll have time to go back up to the moor to cut some more to replace it. Let's light a fire before it starts raining again."

The cattle and ponies dropped their heads to eat as soon as they had crossed the river, and were cropping hungrily at the grass. Satisfied all was well with them, Yrwen left them eating happily, and she and Cavan worked together with their firestone and twigs to get a fire going. Dara backed off. "I'll go up back onto the moor and cut some turf," she offered, taking up the back bag and emptying the precious bulrush tubers onto a stone, along with the fishing net.

"Sure you'll be all right?" Cavan called after her, watching the small figure cross the busy stream and climb wearily back the way they had just come.

"Yes," Dara called back briefly. Anarhys watched her go.

"Dara doesn't like fire," Yrwen told them. "He seems to be genuinely scared of it. He's a bit odd. I mean, fire's so important. What's the problem?"

"Maybe he was badly burned when he was small," Cavan suggested. "Lots of children fall into fire. Some people have horribly scarred faces. Maybe he's scarred from it under his clothes where we can't see it."

Anarhys did not answer. There had been no burn scars on Dara's body. He watched Dara go off alone with some anxiety, and, trying not to appear concerned, he took the fishing net out and spread it on the ground. About eighteen inches long and twelve wide, it had been made with fine twisted grasses, and covered with pitch to keep it waterproof. He had brought it on the journey, thinking it would prove to be more useful than fish hooks. He and Cavan would stretch it across the stream to catch freshwater fish, which they could cook with the tubers for a meal. There was a lot to do tonight before they could sleep, but they had made good time, and they could have a decent break at the campsite with some proper food, and make a start tomorrow at dawn for the Gogarth Headland.

★★★

The entrance to the bay below the village that Grey Wolf had identified for his attack was well protected by sloping cliffs and rocky reefs, but there was an isolated, sandy landing place about a mile before they reached it. As his crews disembarked Grey Wolf ordered his men to make a camp at the top of the beach, but on no account should they build a fire. He was confident that his flotilla had arrived onshore unseen. They could make their way along the coast in the dark, and attack the village at night. Under no circumstances were they going to give themselves away. The people of Gwrtheyrn village needed to be fast asleep when they arrived.

Chapter Nine

"We need to get going," Anarhys called to the other three as the cool grey dawn met them next morning. He felt safer from the night Spirits than he had for some time, knowing that other Humans had been there before him. There was an unexpected feeling of satisfaction as he looked around at the camp site, a sensation he hadn't felt for days. They had woken up in dry clothes which had dried in the wind before nightfall; the precious ponies and cattle, looking fit and well, were grazing unconcernedly close by; the fire showed signs of being alive under its topping of turf.

For once he had slept well. Last night the rain had stayed away, the fire lit easily, the net had caught small silver fish, and Dara had returned from the moor with a bag full of flawlessly cut peat to dry by the fire. She was accompanied by two young men whom she had met on the path, and they were also on their way to do business on the Gogarth Headland. They had left their mountain village in order to bring sheep to trade, and these were now mixed in among their own animals, diligently cropping the turf. They were less valuable than cattle but the Gogarth People would be doubtless glad enough of them for their wool. Anarhys had chosen to trust the two boys, and they had shared the fire, the food and conversation for the evening.

"Ask them if they want to come with us," Anarhys said to Yrwen as they prepared to move on in the morning light. He hoped they would, and that all six of them would cross the isthmus of the Headland together with their animals. Approaching the mining area with its formidable tribe of people would be less daunting with six people ready to trade than just four. He was to be disappointed. Yrwen crossed to the two sleeping shapes and pushed them mercilessly with her foot. "Are you coming on with us?"

"What's the hurry?" a muffled young voice replied. "You go. We'll come on later and meet you at the mine."

"Your ewes might follow us," Yrwen pointed out.

"Send them back if they do," came the muffled voice again, the body still unmoving.

"Typical unhelpful young men," muttered Yrwen. "Oh, not you, Dara," she added as she spotted Dara up, well away from the fire and checking the livestock.

Anarhys smiled to himself, but a little wryly. It was astonishing to him that Yrwen and Cavan had still not noticed that Dara was female, living so closely together as they all did. She disappeared to see to her personal needs when the rest of them were thinking only of their immediate surroundings, and they hadn't noticed anything unusual. Anarhys hadn't yet found the moment to talk to Dara about it. He wondered when he ever would.

Cavan damped down the fire with peat, and gathered

up the remains of last night's cooking. "Not much for breakfast. Cold fish with sorrel, watercress, drop of milk," he said, handing it out. We should get some food at Gogarth. It was fun having the company of those two young fellows, wasn't it? They were full of stories. Pity they can't get up in the morning and come with us."

"They had some great tales," agreed Yrwen. "Their people from the great mountain range may be poor, but they've seen some action. Having your sheep rustled must be a nightmare."

"I know," said Anarhys. "Awful. We have our Ancestors to thank for living by the sea. Making a living in the mountains must be even harder than near the shore." He looked at his surroundings and his feeling of satisfaction rapidly evaporated at the thought of what lay ahead. The landscape looked unfriendly. Although they had left the open moors behind them, the mountains of their own Ancestors were further away than ever, and nearby the Gogarth Headland reared up, crowned with smoke, in the sombre, unfamiliar ocean. He kept thinking longingly of his home village – the four round houses; twenty-five villagers, young and old; the reddish cattle; the calf; the two hill ponies and scattering of sheep up on the hillsides; their mountain which slid down into the sea behind the settlement; the two fields of barley. He was beginning to feel real apprehension at the tasks he had undertaken, and he longed for the day to be over and for them all to be on their way home again. With or without Yrwen.

They spent precious minutes separating the cattle and ponies from their visitors' sheep, then herded them along the deeply well-worn track towards the Headland.

Before they descended to the start of the low isthmus that attached Gogarth Headland to the mainland Anarhys called a halt. He wanted to survey the land ahead and make a plan.

"I can remember that the track crosses the isthmus and goes on up to the village," he said. "The village is at the base of that sloping cliff at the other end, and we have to go through it and then climb the slope behind to get to the trading post. The mines and bronze factory lie further up, near the top of the Headland, but obviously we won't be allowed anywhere near it. We'll get as far as the trading post and do our business with the cows first, Dara. Then when that's done we can help you with your ponies." He wondered what she was thinking and glanced into her face, but there were no clues. She was silent and her face unreadable.

"The Ancestors will be able to see us from our mountains," Cavan observed, to strengthen everybody's resolve, and he believed it absolutely, even if Anarhys didn't. "The Spirits have let us come this far. We'll have good trading. It will all turn out well and we'll be on our way home tonight."

"Do you think we should make the Spirits another offering?" Yrwen asked.

"Only when we've finished," said Cavan. "We can walk back along the shore of the isthmus and make an offering to the Spirits in the sea to thank them."

"It'll be good to be on our way home," said Yrwen. "Father will be pleased to see us. I wonder if anything much is happening at home in Gwrtheyrn."

Anarhys was saying to himself yet again – Thank goodness Cavan is with me. He understands the Spirit world so well. I don't know what I'd do without him. But he'd never let me leave Yrwen here. She'll have to come back to Gwrtheyrn with us. It will only make everything even more difficult during our time on Gogarth to do anything about finding her a husband. He thought the isthmus was wider that he remembered – about half a mile across. When he had crossed it with his father Iago all those years ago the grass had been fresh and green, the sun had given freely of its light and warmth, and there had been pale blue harebells nodding their heads, sulphur yellow rock roses, shy mauve self-heal growing among the green. The whirr of flying insects had been loud in his ears, and there were the scents of pollen, dry earth and stemmy greenness mixed with the saltiness of the sea air. Today the track was a miry pathway which muddied each foot that fell, and the grass either side was damp and brownish. The scents in his nose were of wetness – clammy soil, dank herbage, and moss.

As they crossed the isthmus the earthy smell began to change to that of acrid smoke as it chased out towards the mountains. A mixture of sounds was heard above the wind: human and animal voices, sea birds shrieking into the moving air, and a distant muffled thumping of the mining and working of metals. Anarhys squared his shoulders and walked resolutely forward: "I'll go up front," he said.

"Much bigger than our settlement," observed Yrwen with wonder. "Look at the fence and ditch round it. They must have brought that timber in from miles away. And all their livestock. Their houses aren't old and decrepit like ours, and most of them are big enough to have porches on them. They must be wealthy trading all that bronze. I can smell meat cooking," she added after a moment, with some longing.

"Odd time to be cooking meat, first thing in the morning," Cavan remarked. "Must have been roasting all night. I expect they saw us coming and thought they'd feed us so we'd be in a better mood to deal. They would have known we'd be hungry. And tired." The track had become a droveway running between small paddocks divided by low stone walls. There was a field of young barley, and areas grazed by cattle and sheep which foraged on the wet sward. They were hardy, ancient livestock which did well on poor grazing; evidently they were used to passing strangers because they didn't raise their heads to look at the travellers. The droveway was surfaced with alder logs pegged horizontally, forming a solid track which invited travellers to walk on it. After the clinging mud they were only too glad to do so.

The track steered them through the wooden portal of the surrounding fence, and at last they were in the village. Anarhys looked around at a settlement scene very unlike his own. The men and women here still wore clothes dyed in different colours – yellow from camomile and tansy, blues and pinks from sea snails. Some of the women wore dresses with shining metal ornaments. Their hair was clean and neat, their faces were not grey and gaunt like his own people's faces, but well fed and lived-in. Their movements were bright and confident, unlike those of his own weary people. Three children who had been playing and laughing by a roundhouse approached curiously but without trepidation, and even the village dogs looked sleek and at ease. It was very unlike Anarhys' expectation of a wild and fierce people. A few villagers paused in their work to admire Dara's blue pony.

Three sturdy Gogarth men stood on the track in front of them, barring their way. They didn't look wild, but there was a severely uncompromising attitude in their faces. Loosely held in their hands were bronze-tipped spears. Anarhys eyed the glittering metal; he fought hard with himself not to be alarmed by its power, and forced himself to assume the virtue of strength. Instead he bid them Good day.

"Good day," returned the oldest of the Gogarth Men, and he had a strangely lilting, ominous voice. There was another man at each of his shoulders. Without a pause he added, "I am Owain, Village Chief and Head Trader of Gogarth. You have come with goods to trade." It was not a question.

"Yes," said Anarhys, and was silent, reminding himself to say as little as possible.

"Then come with me," the man told him, and led them on through the village. Anarhys followed, striding out with what he hoped was confidence. Dara came after him, Blue nodding her head at her shoulder, the dun pressing close. The cattle followed dutifully, then Yrwen and Cavan, thankful for each other's company, and with the black dog between them. The two Gogarth men fell back in behind. They left the village from the timber portal on the opposite side and together headed up the barren scarp slope and onto the Gogarth Headland itself.

The Headland spread out before the group as they reached the top of the slope, and despite the fatigue and hunger that was overtaking them again they looked at it in speculation. It rose gently to the summit about a mile away in front of them, a foreland of peat clad in damp heather, and dotted with sheep. The gloomy sky was darkened with smoke from the smelting peat fires, and the heavy sounds of the working mine were louder now they were so close. From this point the cheerless sea was out of sight, but its waves could be heard thudding dully against the cliffs below. There was no doubt in anybody's mind that Spirits here were hostile.

The trading post was set out well away from the entrance to the mine and factory, so that no visitor might observe the supernatural mysteries of the ore being extracted from the earth, or its miraculous and incredible metamorphosis into living metal artefacts. Dara and Cavan would never see over the edge of the huge bowl-shaped depression where it lay, or observe the dark holes leading from it into the unfathomable depths of the earth. Few pairs of eyes knew of the smoke escaping through the reed roof of the stone-built smelting house, the giant cooling water troughs, the heaps of jade-green malachite ore, or the great piles of spoil and broken clay casts. The bronze smiths themselves, immensely muscular, soot-covered, red-eyed, their arms covered in heat-protective sheepskins as they worked the precious metals were the arcane sect of people who knew the secrets. These were the wild Gogarth men Anarhys had been expecting to see, but they kept themselves well hidden.

What he did see at the trading post were bronze items laid out on a table, each burnished to a gleaming greyish silver. Anarhys looked closer, still standing a little back to give them the respect they deserved. There were three astonishingly beautiful crafted swords, each about fifteen inches long, leaf-bladed, with a strong central rib, and rivets for attaching a hilt. They had all been cast in the same style, and were undoubtedly made as high status symbols for men of great power. Few of those sort of men were left now: any tribal leaders Anarhys knew of were struggling for existence just as Iago was. There were arrowheads and spear heads, the arrowheads, similar to the ones Anarhys had already seen, frighteningly sharpened, with flush sockets and curved edges; but Anarhys and Yrwen were not interested in weapons. There were bright new knife blades of different sizes, and meat hooks designed for pulling meat and fish out of hot water pits, but Anarhys ignored those: he would replace his knife later and they had meat hooks of their own at home. There were a few ladies' dress fastenings in the shape of two circles joined by a miniature metal rope, and he allowed himself a fanciful moment imagining Dara wearing one on a coloured cloak like the people of Gogarth Village. He pushed the thought from his head. Who could buy such luxuries in these times? It was working farm implements they needed. There were axe heads of different sizes which Dara would need later, and to his relief he saw several shining sickles. He tried to appear as a good trader might, as if he didn't care, wasn't tired or hungry, and wouldn't mind going home empty-handed if the deals didn't suit him. He watched from the corner of his eye as Cavan and Dara took the ponies away and left Yrwen and himself to do business with Owain over the two cows.

"What is it you have come for?" Owain asked him.

"Well, I might be looking for sickles," said Anarhys after a moment.

"What about these?"

Resisting the urge to shout "Perfect!" Anarhys glanced at them, and courageously took one of them into his hands. He could feel the power in the metal, but he attempted to see beyond this at the tool itself. It was made for service, not for looks, and weighed heavily in his hand. He remembered the advice Caersws had given him by the river, and avoiding the sharpness of the edge, squeezed it in his fingers. It felt cool and strong. "How much tin is in it?" he asked.

"Just the right amount. And a drop of lead. We are experts. We make the best bronze in the country," Owain told him, a persuasive dealer.

"And the price?"

"Your two cows for two sickles. You will need to take two. One is not enough. You will need to sharpen one while the other is in use." Owain had been inspecting the two cows critically. He was aware that one was in milk and was a high-value commodity.

Anarhys was silent, thinking. "We need food and a night's sleep," he said after a moment.

"We can give you a meal of roasted ox, and we have ale. And you may stay one night in the village."

Ale! Roast ox! Anarhys felt like leaping for joy at the thought of a full belly, drink to ease his worries, and at least one night sleeping under a roof, even if it was with strangers. Maybe he could even up the stakes and make it two nights, and look out for a husband for Yrwen. Yet he needed to get home to Iago. The thought of his father made him look towards the mountain summits far away in the distance. As ever the peaks were invisible, hidden by clouds, but he thought the mists were thinning.

"What do you think, Yrwen?" he asked her quietly, stepping away from Owain to confer with her.

"I think we should agree, but only on the condition that we are all fed and rested before we deal with Dara's ponies, and that we do his trading later this afternoon. And," Yrwen went on after a moment's thought, "that they should throw into the deal something that we can offer the Spirits as a sacrifice, and that they provide us with breakfast tomorrow morning."

Anarhys paused again, this time for longer. Yrwen's suggestions made sense, but was it too much to ask for? He wished Cavan was standing nearer to him, not away up the hill with Dara. He wondered what his Ancestors would want him to do. As he did so he realised that some of the bronze goods he was being shown – the swords, the attractive jewellery – would probably never be traded in these terrible times of shortages. Who could afford them? Nobody. The exchange Yrwen suggested seemed fair to him. Mentally he asked for Iago's blessing, then turned to Owain.

"The young cow is still milking, she is worth extra," said Anarhys with a new confidence. "As well as the sickles we should like a good meal, a bed tonight, and for luck you can throw in an item that we can use as an offering for the Spirits."

There was an even longer pause.

Anarhys' heart picked up tempo as he waited for Owain's reply.

It came at last. "You are asking a lot. However, in exchange for your two cows you may have two bronze sickle, a meal now, a safe night's sleep in our village, and breakfast tomorrow morning, but nothing more. Not items for an offering to the Spirits. Then this afternoon we can do business with the ponies."

Anarhys was unsure how to react. He stood absolutely still. He felt the ground cool under his feet, heard the wind blowing across the grasses and the mewling gulls. He was aware of his woollen clothes touching his skin and closed his eyes. Time stilled for him, but when he opened his eyes again a few seconds later he had his reply ready.

"We agree," said Anarhys, and he and Yrwen each shook Owain's hard, muscular hand.

When he had shaken Yrwen's hand, Owain picked up a small bronze disc from among the items on trading post. Anarhys wondered whether Owain was going to give it to Yrwen as luck money after all, but instead the village chief carried the treasure up onto the top of the hill and paused on the skyline. Watching him, Anarhys knew suddenly what he was going to do. There must be water up there, and Owain was giving the bronze to the Water Spirit as an offering of thanks. There were a few minutes while the figure on the skyline seemed to speak to the Spirits, then he was seen to cast his offering reverently.

"No drinking ale at the meal," said Anarhys to Yrwen. "Not if we have to help Dara trade this afternoon. We can indulge in the morning."

"Quite," said Yrwen.

★★★

Several hours later, fed, well-rested, feeling physically better, but free of alcohol, Dara and Anarhys stood at the trading post with Owain.

Yrwen and Cavan sat close together up the hill from the trading post. Cavan was holding Yrwen's hand.

Chapter Ten

"Which one of these will it be, Dara?" Anarhys asked as they looked down at three bronze axes lying together in a semi-circle on the rough yellow blanket. The shining bronze showed up sharply against its rough weave, the cruel curved blades a few inches in length, handles ready hafted.

"All of them."

"Very difficult to manufacture," said Owain. "Only the best and most experienced craftsmen can work axes. They use a lot of metal and take a long time to cast without a risk of breaking. The handles are made of hazel, and they are the best you will ever see." He was not looking at the blue pony as he said this, but at Anarhys and Dara, although they both knew he had been watching Blue with appraising eyes since their arrival. He wanted Blue badly. With her remarkable size and unusual colouring, ownership of such an animal would increase his status even more. Both ponies were grazing unconcernedly a few yards away.

Anarhys picked up an axe, weighing it in his hand, and he could feel the life breathing in the metal. He ran his thumb along the arching blade and it was frighteningly sharp. He was sure that using a tool like this, alive with earth Spirits, would make the work of cutting timber quicker and easier. And in times of need Mabin could always give such a magnificent object as a votive offering to the Water Spirits.

"Which one for the dun pony?" Dara asked Owain.

"I will take both your ponies for one axe."

"My blue pony as well?"

"Both ponies."

Dara looked mutinous, but to Anarhys' relief she said nothing. Remembering Caersws' advice, he inspected the handle of the axe in his hand. It had been carefully fashioned from a single piece of timber where a branch had grown out at right angles, and it was smooth, free of a single crack or blemish, and highly polished to prevent splintering the skin. Closing his fist round it, he could feel its strength, and his fingers were a perfect fit on the cool wood. It fitted snugly into the socket, and was secured tightly with leather thread as Caersws had advised. Immediately he felt at one with the tool, as though it was a part of his arm. He handed it to Dara reluctantly, disinclined to let go of its pleasing feel.

"Try this," he said to her.

Dara took the axe from him. Because of the perfect craftsmanship it fitted into her small hand just as easily as it had Anarhys', and straight away she felt the same affinity with it that Anarhys had. It was almost as though the tool had come home to her. She walked away for a few steps and swung it at a tuft of rank grass. The blade sliced through as though it was air. She went back to the table and tried the other two axes with the same result. When she had replaced them on the table she was silent, looking into the distance towards the mountains in the east.

The silence lasted for some time. Anarhys could hear again the sounds of the isolated Gogarth Headland lying out in the sea: the crying sea birds, the wind in the sodden grasses, and the hammering and human voices from the copper mine away up on the hill. He went over to Dara and said in a very low voice so Owain didn't hear, "What do you think, Dara?"

Equally quietly, "The axes are good. They're just what we need."

"Do you want to do the deal with Owain?"

"I want the axe," said Dara, a trifle stubbornly.

"So what about the deal then?"

"He can have my dun pony. Not Blue."

Owain walked away. He could not hear what was being said, but he wanted to give Dara and Anarhys time to discuss things. And he didn't want to appear avaricious about Blue.

"Owain will not trade an axe for just one pony, Dara. If you need an axe you'll have to trade in Blue as well."

"No."

"Why not?"

"He can't have Blue. She's mine. I trained her. She knows me. She wouldn't like to stay here among those rough men. She wants to come home to Ddu Village with me." With each sentence her voice was raised.

Anarhys was shocked. "What would Caersws and your father say if you went home with Blue, and no axe? Your journey would have been pointless," he said, managing to keep his voice down, and remain reasonable.

"I don't know, but the Gogarth people can't have Blue. She's my best friend. I couldn't go home without her."

Anarhys looked hard at Dara, willing her to see reason, feeling both exasperation and compassion for her. This young girl, an odd person, but full of fierce protection for the pony which she described as her best friend, was powerless against Owain. He had told Caersws he would help her, but if she wouldn't let Blue go she was beyond his help. He felt weighed down with frustration. Mabin's tribe were relying on her trading well; their lives might depend on acquiring the axe. He tried again.

"Dara," he said, "you need the axe. It may be the difference between survival and starvation for your village. You must do the deal. Yrwen let her cows go. You must let Blue go too."

"I can't, Anarhys. I can't leave Blue here. She'd be frightened here with the Gogarth People."

"She'd be fine," said Anarhys, his anxiety rising.

Owain wandered back to them. "What are your thoughts?" he asked.

"You can have the dun pony for that axe," said Dara obstinately, pointing to the best of the tools before her.

"Both your ponies for the axe," said Owain imperturbably.

Dara and Owain looked at each other across a seemingly impassable space. Neither would give way. Anarhys watched helplessly as Dara, with her copper-coloured hair blowing damply round her head, her grey-green eyes and pale face, stood her ground. There was silence between them all. Anarhys was desperate to help Dara, but couldn't think how. He was more agitated than she was. Then he remembered how the answer had come to him over his own deal with Owain. He stood quite still, hearing the sounds of Gogarth, feeling the wind on his face and in his hair, the ground cool beneath his feet, smelling the damp grass and the sea air. He felt his clothes touching his body. His mind became still, and in the emptiness he had his answer. Reaching into his tunic, he felt for his money belt. His fingers closed on the gold disc his father has given him back at Gwrtheyrn. It was warm and comforting where it has been nestling against his skin. He drew it out stealthily, absolutely certain he had to do this for Dara.

Very slowly Anarhys opened his fingers out to Owain, revealing the glowing deep yellow of the elegant object in the palm of his hand. Owain gave a visible start, took his eyes of Dara, and stepped forward to look. Still nothing was said, but as the gold gleamed hypnotically out at them Owain bent his head still closer to it, transfixed by its beauty.

"It's pure gold from the mines at Halkyn," said Anarhys at last.

"Prove to me that it's real gold."

"See that mark on it? It's soft metal. It's pure all right," Anarhys told Owain.

There was an altered silence between Anarhys and Owain, now that each had a new expectation. To his discomfort, Anarhys saw Yrwen from the corner of his eye coming down the hill to them.

"What's going on?" Yrwen asked, then saw the gleaming gold lying in Anarhys' hand. "That's one of our mother's brooches. What are you doing with it, Anarhys?

You can't be using it to trade with? This is Dara's deal. It's nothing to do with us."

"Dara won't part with the Blue pony," Anarhys told her.

"I don't care. You can't use Mother's jewellery to trade for him."

"Dara can't go home without an axe."

"Yes, he can. Don't do it, Anarhys." Yrwen was distressed.

Owain took over for a moment. Seeing the lovely object might not come his way after all, he said quickly "My best axe for your gold sun disc and the dun pony."

"I agree," said Anarhys, and avoiding his sister's eye as Owain held his hand out, he tipped the glowing piece onto its palm. Owain's fingers closed round it, and the lovely object was gone.

They shook hands.

★★★

Anarhys watched Owain and his two companions take the dun pony down towards the village, leaving a guard to watch at the bronze trading point. Safely in his back bag were the two bronze sickles, and in Dara's hands was the axe, but the gold disc had gone. Beside him stood Yrwen, shaking with anger and white-faced, with the faithful black dog lying by her legs. Cavan joined her, and put his arm round her shoulders hoping to calm her. Dara remained in the background, standing close to Blue.

"What on earth did you do that for?" stormed Yrwen to Anarhys. "The gold belongs to our tribe, not Dara's. How can we go back to Father without it?"

"Dara's tribe needs that axe. Don't you see, Yrwen? She won't leave Blue here and she can't go back to Mabin without an axe."

Yrwen heard Anarhys refer to Dara as "she", but in the heat of the moment it didn't register. "You shouldn't have done it," she said, still very angry.

Cavan tried to placate her. "It's done now, Yrwen. Let's get down to the village and have some food. And look, the sky's lightening. The clouds are thinning." And for some reason he added quietly into her ear, "It'll be all right."

He and Anarhys wrapped the sickles carefully in the empty body belt that had protected the golden disc, and returned it to the back pack. As Cavan bent down he felt an icy chill prickle his back. He pulled his hood over his head, imagining the raw Gogarth wind had burrowed down the back of his tunic. The coldness was still there. He put down the bag and stood up. Still there. Something was wrong, something was warning him. He looked out over the grim grey sea, but there was nothing unusual to see. He glanced into the bag.

"What is it, Cavan?" asked Anarhys, catching the familiar inward-looking expression on Cavan's face that told him his friend's ability to see things happening elsewhere was at work.

"I'm not sure. I don't know what it is, but something's not right. Let's wait for a bit and take stock before we go down to the village. Then we can ask for something to wrap Dara's axe in to travel home, and get something to eat." Cavan shook himself, wondering to himself whether his premonition would return, then added more cheerfully, "I can smell that meat roasting from here. It's good. The Gogarth people must have seen us coming."

Dara stood with her hand on Blue a little way away, feeling awkward. She had heard Yrwen blaming her for losing the gold in the negotiations, but there was nothing she could do about it, and she felt excluded; she simply wanted to be back in her own village. Yrwen was telling herself that without Dara they would all be safely on their way home with the bronze by now, and she looked back across the isthmus which was the path to Gwrtheyrn. Cavan and Anarhys gathered themselves together to follow Owain down the slope to Gogarth Village. They were all facing west, back the way they had come, across the isthmus of the Gogarth Headland, and towards the mountains. Smoke from the smelting oven at the mine head across the hill them stung their eyes, but they could all see in the distance little biscuit-coloured blobs coming along the path from the Mainland towards the village.

"It's the boys with the sheep who shared our fire last night," said Anarhys.

"So it is. Look Yrwen," said Cavan, and found he was still shaking from his earlier chill.

"What is it, Cavan?" asked Anarhys again.

"Really, nothing," Cavan repeated. "I'm just cold."

He was mistaken about there being nothing wrong, but correct about the clouds thinning. As the four watched the little flock of sheep bobbing along the track they saw the summits of the mountains behind were starting to lose their cloaking mists.

Two of them were crowned with fiery beacons.

★★★

With a quick intake of breath Anarhys stood up. He felt light-headed as he remembered both Iago's and Mabin's cautions to him about the Iron Men, and how he had treated their warnings with scorn. Now he did not feel nearly so confident. Yrwen saw the fires and was startled into immobility. Gone instantly were her furious thoughts about Anarhys and Dara. Her head felt numb with astonishment.

The Gogarth People were taking the warning signal very seriously indeed. A man was already running up the heathery hillside to the head of the mine, and when he reached it he gave a shout and disappeared straight over the brink, down into the hollow where the bronzesmiths were working. Anarhys watched as he carried the shocking news of the lighted beacons to the workers. With the people of Gogarth occupied by their own concerns there was nobody to spot Anarhys as he took the opportunity to make his way over to the hollow in the ground where the mine head was situated and look down into it. He saw the workers stop their movements, and become frozen in time as the news was given to them. He watched the messenger hasten to the black mine entrance and disappear into the darkness within.

The muscled bronzesmiths worked rapidly to extinguish their fires. Great stone beakers of water doused the flames, charcoal fuel was pulled out from the glowing red centres, and leather hides were thrown over and held down hard to stop air entering and re-igniting. They were giving nobody the chance of discovering the presence of their precious copper mine through its smoke. Stone hammers and bronze axes were taken up and used to smash their smelting tools – stone crucibles for heating the metal alloys in the fire, clay moulds for casting the bronze, even the giant wooden bellows, which only a minute ago had been used for heating the fires to intense temperatures, were shattered by mighty blows. They were leaving, but nothing would be left behind for their enemies.

Not even their slaves. A different race of people began to shuffle from the blackness of the mines. They were men, women and small children, pale-skinned, thin, and bent after a lifetime of working ore from low airless tunnels in the pale glow of candles. They tried to hurry, but they could only shamble, peering blindly in the sudden light and tripping on smashed objects as they crossed the bowl of the mine head. Ignoring Anarhys they climbed up over the edge onto the Headland and headed dispiritedly down towards the Gogarth village.

The smiths, satisfied that they were leaving nothing of the working factory behind, gathered together finished bronze items and stacked them swiftly in leather bags. They carried them up to where Dara, Cavan and Yrwen were standing with the guard who had been with them and quickly took up the bronze items laid out on the wooden trading bench, adding them to their bags. Without a word they carried them away towards their village. One sword remained, gleaming on the bench.

The last man stayed behind, took hold of it, and made his way up to where Owain had been standing as he made an offering to the Spirits. Anarhys, still at the mine head, watched him. Without so much as pausing to break the blade or part it from its handle, the bronzesmith knelt on the ground. When he stood up again the sword had gone. He followed his fellow-smiths down towards Gogarth village empty-handed.

The mine had been stilled and silenced so completely that the Headland seemed more isolated than ever. "There are women coming up the hill from the village," observed Yrwen in the quietness. "They're running. What are they doing?"

"They're coming to round the sheep up," guessed Cavan. "There are dogs with them."

Anarhys hurried back to where the trading post had been so recently active. "I still can't see any boats coming in from the sea, but the Gogarth people are taking the beacons unbelievably seriously," he observed, straining his eyes out over the grey waters, searching for signs of danger. "I suppose we should go too. I wonder how much time we have."

They all looked at Cavan, hoping his powers could help them.

"I can't tell," Cavan said helplessly after a few moments. "I honestly don't know. But we must move on."

A small voice by Anarhys said, "Some of the Gogarth villagers have left and started across the isthmus towards the mountains." It was Dara. She had moved in closer to Anarhys to gain strength from the group's numbers and was watching what was happening at the village below them. Blue was grazing near her.

"We ought to get going. We've got to get the bronze across to the mainland as fast as we can," said Yrwen.

Anarhys thought – it's propitious that we still have Dara's pony. She could be really useful. Perhaps if we offer the Spirits something now to acknowledge Blue they will help us again. I know there's a peat hole up on the hill where the Spirits live because I've seen both the Gogarth village chief and the bronzesmith make an offering there.

"You know, if there's danger, we have nothing to defend ourselves with," Cavan observed. "Apart from our knives. No spearheads, no swords. There's nothing left at the minehead. The bronzesmiths took absolutely everything."

"Anarhys, we should go," said Yrwen again. "We don't need weapons, Cavan. They'd only hold us up. We need to get home."

"I know we do. Perhaps we should climb down and cross the isthmus to the mainland down along the seashore, not along the path at the top," went on Cavan. "That way we wouldn't be seen so easily from the sea."

"Good idea, we'll do that, Cavan. And you're right, we don't have weapons for protecting ourselves." Anarhys could hardly believe that the tales of the Iron Men, disdainfully dismissed only a few days ago, were now becoming a threatening reality.

"We wouldn't know how to use them anyway," Yrwen said. "We're isolated, peaceful people, just trying to farm enough to eat and trade a bit. There are so few of us in the countryside we've never had to defend our land."

"We learned how to fight as children," returned Cavan. "The men who had been away at war in the East showed us."

"But we were just playing with sticks," said Yrwen, agitated by the way the conversation was leading.

Anarhys, feeling felt less uncertain of himself now that he had been justified in retaining Dara's blue pony, said, "We do need to get home quickly. But it would be better to have a weapon. Just in case we have to defend ourselves. I've had an idea. I'm going up to the top of the Headland, then we'll go. Come with me, Cavan."

Chapter Eleven

I'll go too," said Yrwen. "Let's all go. We'll get a better view of the sea from the top, and if that's where the danger's coming from we might see exactly what it is. You'd better come as well, Dara, so we all stay together. But then we must leave the Gogarth Headland and get away." Dara, pleased to be included in arrangements again, followed Anarhys, Yrwen and Cavan up the hillside.

Even in the grey atmosphere and eternal clouds of the times, the view from the crest of the Gogarth's Headland was like a glimpse into infinity. The prominence they were standing on, almost an island, was set in the bleak open ocean, and they could see out in every direction. To the west was the mystical and holy island of Mon, a reminder of the spiritual life of the country, lying flatly on the horizon. To the south was the mainland, the moors and mountains practically at the sea's edge, the beacons still alight on the summits. To the north and east was nothing but water as far as they could see.

"I can't see anything on the sea," said Yrwen.

"It's difficult to make out boats against the waves

and the colour of the sea," said Cavan, looking hard. "Sometimes I think I see something, then it disappears." He remembered his vision of the little black dots on the sea, but kept it to himself. Some things didn't need to be said.

"There are those women with the dogs," Dara said. "They've got to the end of the Headland."

They stood on the top of the Headland and watched the distant figures. At the far end the women spread out to form a straight line across the width of the peninsular. They walked quickly back towards the Gogarth village, gathering before them sheep and goats which had been grazing there. Not a word was said between them, their line never faltered, and the dogs worked obediently between them. The exercise was run with military precision. The sheep ran forward together through the heather in front of them, bleating anxiously and racing each other as they picked up speed. They passed below Anarhys and his companions standing motionless at the summit, by-passed the copper mine lying below them, skipped nimbly down the slope, and were funnelled through the timber portal into the village. They could be seen bunched up together and moving rapidly through the main street of the village, out through the far portal, and onto the track that crossed the top of the isthmus. It had taken only a few minutes.

In silence the group standing on the highest point of the Headland saw the village vacated. Fires were extinguished just as they had been up at the copper mine. Cattle and ponies were herded out of the little fields, and sent off along the track way leading back to the mainland. Possessions were loaded onto wooden carts and oxen were harnessed to them to drag them after the cattle. Small figures – the village children – were carried or walked through the portal on their way towards the mountains and the dogs accompanied them. Nobody doubled back. No animal or person was left behind. The exodus was complete. Anarhys, Yrwen, Cavan and Dara were abandoned on the Gogarth Headland with its alien Spirits. Yrwen's dog, Dara's pony and the seagulls crying and riding on the wind were their only companions.

"That whole thing was just unbelievable," Dara said slowly in the quietness that followed.

"Extraordinary," agreed Cavan. "The tribe simply must have been rehearsing it. They knew there was danger. Even the sheep knew where to go."

"They should have warned us," said Yrwen. "But at least we've done the deals and got the stuff we wanted. Thankfully we didn't wait for the boys at the campsite this morning, or we'd have been too late and be going back empty-handed."

"Probably that's why the traders didn't tell us," reasoned Anarhys. "They might have thought we'd go back without doing business if we knew. Less bronze for them to carry, and they got the cattle and pony. In any case, I don't expect we'd have believed them even if they had told us."

"Anarhys, we must…" began Yrwen.

"Won't be a minute, Yrwen. I just need to find something. You go on with Dara if you like. I can catch you up." Anarhys, eyes to the ground, was taking a few steps in every direction, stopping and checking, then walking again.

"What are you looking for?" Dara and Cavan asked together.

"There's a pool up here which I saw Owain use for offering gifts to the Spirits. See if you can find it. I know it's round here somewhere because not only did Owain present it with bronze when we had traded the cows, but one of the smiths came up here with a bronze sword and it looked to me as though that went in too. There must be water around," said Anarhys.

"What on earth d'you want with a pool?" said Yrwen. "We're not going to give any offerings yet. We need to get off the Headland before we do that. Come on, Anarhys. Let's get away while we can. Tell him, Cavan."

Cavan watched Anarhys' resolute face and knew he was serious. "Why do you need sacred water?" he asked.

Anarhys didn't answer. He was preoccupied in his search of the ground around them. It was the black dog that found the peat hole full of cold brown water. Feeling thirsty, it wandered off to look for water, and Dara heard it lapping above the sound of the wind in the heather. She followed the sound, and the dog, finishing his drink, looked up expectantly at her.

"Over here," she shouted to Anarhys. He got to her across the heather as quickly as he could as she stood looking down at the black pool hidden among the herbage. He looked down with her.

"Thank you, Dara," he said.

Anarhys measured the area of water with his eyes and guessed it was about two man-heights along each side. He and Dara gazed onto the water. Its surface was below the level of the soft brown earth, and it lay uncannily still, hardly disturbed by the wind under the darkened skies. The edges were cleanly cut where turf had been sliced out for hundreds of years, and the sides dived perpendicularly into the depths. The water was a deep peaty brown for the first few inches, but after that it was utterly, threateningly black. Anarhys and Dara, standing on the edge, felt as though they were looking into the entrance to the underworld. They had no idea what lay below the blackness.

Anarhys knelt down by the pool and put his head down to look as closely as he could to look into the dark waters. Thinking of all the offerings that must have been cast into the peat hole over the years he thought it might be possible to see a tiny gleam of bronze where something had chanced to catch on a ledge and not fallen all the way to the bottom. He searched hard, but there was nothing. Anything placed there must have sunk out of sight.

"What are you doing?" asked Dara.

"I'm looking to see if I can see the sword the bronzesmith left here. If I can get it out we could take it with us," replied Anarhys. He was hoping to secure her admiration when he said this. There would probably be protestation too, but not without awe.

"No Anarhys!" Dara cried, horrified. "You can't take votive offerings back from the Spirits. Think how They might take revenge!"

Yrwen and Cavan raced over.

"He wants to take bronze out of a sacred pool," she told them frantically.

"Don't be stupid, Anarhys," stormed Yrwen. "Whatever are you thinking about? Of course you can't do that."

Anarhys said nothing. Cavan watched him. He had never seen his friend look this determined before, and he didn't think he would be able to stop Anarhys doing whatever it was he was going to do. He glanced into the peat hole and tried to see it from Anarhys' point of view – not as an entrance to the world of the Spirits, a sanctified place, but as a watery hole which might give up a treasure for them. It was impossible for him. Cavan's belief in the Spirits was absolute and unshakeable, and he simply looked into the water with deep foreboding.

Drops of rain were beginning to fall again, causing annular wrinkles on its smooth surface. Pulling up the sleeve of his woollen tunic, Anarhys reached his arm into the still waters, testing the freezing temperature. The other three watched in dismay. Yrwen reached down and grabbed his arm.

"Stop it," she shouted at him. "Don't do that. Think what Father would say. He'd be outraged."

Anarhys gently pulled Yrwen's hand off his arm. He wasn't sure himself why he was so obsessed with what was in the peat hole, but he knew it was something to do with showing his authority in the face of danger, and he especially wanted Dara to see him doing so. He had been disturbed by the loss when his precious, personal knife had been sacrificed earlier at the river crossing, and had been asking himself whether the Spirits really needed all these tangible sacrifices which They could not actually use. He stood up on the damp bank and pulled his tunic off over his head, leaving it in a heap on the grass. Leggings and shoes followed.

He sat down at the edge of the pool with his feet in the water, feeling the bitter cold of its static peatiness.

He looked at Cavan. "Watch out for me," he said, and slid the rest of his body in. Immediately he felt the chill creep into his skin. He gasped and looked about him. Over the lip of the pool he could see his friends standing above him, white-faced and motionless. Behind them were the tips of the mountain summits on the mainland, but other than that his world was made up of the thickly clouded sky above him and the freezing watery element about him. He had no idea of the depth of black water below his body – it could reach into the earth for ever as far as he knew. He suspected not, but it was still a frightening thought. He took a gulp of air and slipped under the surface.

He knew the risks of this exploit full well – the cramps that might drown him, the cold that might render him unconscious, the awful confusion if went so far down into the water that he lost his sense of direction and could not find the surface again, the chance that he might not be able to climb out of the pool when he had finished in the water. In the pitch blackness he felt his way down the spongy wall with his hands, keeping the light of the sky above his head to give direction. There were no ledges in the wall where objects might have caught, no holes or rough bits that might trap something falling, no slopes. It was as straight and smooth as a javelin handle. His ears hurt and his body was squeezed by the pressure of the water. He hadn't reached the bottom where he thought he might find what he was looking for, but the pain became so great that he knew he had to return to the top. Slowly he made his way back through the inkiness towards the light. As his head surfaced he took a great gasp of sweet, precious air.

Yrwen, Cavan and Dara were waiting nervously on the edge to help him out.

"Come on out before you die in there," said Cavan reaching his hand over the water, ready to help him out.

"Please, Anarhys," begged Dara when she saw him, her face grey. "Let's get off the Headland now."

Adrenaline was now racing through Anarhys' body. He was not feeling the cold, only excitement. He forgot the dangers. "I'll just have one more go," he said, and pushed himself away from the bank ready to dive again.

"He'll never find anything," said Yrwen. "He's just wasting time."

"I know," said Cavan. "And I hope he doesn't. But we'll have to wait for him. We can't leave him here."

They watched Anarhys' head disappear again into the fathomless pool. They saw him start down a different side of the peat hole and disappear almost immediately into the gloom. They could not even pray to the Water Spirits for his safe return because they believed he was trespassing in Their element. All they could do was wait.

Anarhys was no longer frightened in the darkness. He might have been blind for all he could see, but he felt his way confidently down the wall. He stayed longer this time, until his lungs were desperate to breathe again. He let out a bubble of air and it slipped past his face unseen. His body longed to be released from the pressure, his ears were roaring and he thought they were ready to burst. He would have to resurface now, his mission failed. Then his hand felt something different. The wall, instead of rising perpendicularly, was sloping, and suddenly it became horizontal. To his astonishment he realized had reached the bottom.

He let another gasp of air from his lungs and checked the small patch of light above his head to get his bearings. All was well. He used both hands to feel for something, anything, that might be lying on the floor of the peat hole; he imagined that so many objects had been thrown into the pool over the years that there must be something. Several moments later a solid metal object, half buried in the bed of the peat hole, lay under his hand. It was a little bronze object, but it was not a knife or a sword. He left it and moved on, his lungs craving air more than ever. He began to imagine there was somebody down here with him, somebody watching him from the walls. He must be hallucinating. There was a stab of fear within him, and as it struck his fingers closed on a rigid metal handle. He tugged it, and it drew freely and invisibly through the water towards him. Not staying to find out what he had hit upon Anarhys carried his prize slowly towards the patch of light above him that was daylight.

It was Cavan who dragged Anarhys over the edge of the peat hole and laid him on the damp turf.

Gasping for air, Anarhys looked at the object in his hand. The other three, distancing themselves from his actions, stood back from him. There was awe in their faces. This was not the uncertain Anarhys they knew. This was somebody who had achieved an amazing feat, whether for good or for evil. The item he was grasping so tightly was a bronze sword.

They looked at his body shivering on the ground, his hair streaming with water. Anarhys's face was blue from the cold, his teeth clattering together, and his eyes half closed. For a moment Cavan wondered whether it was safe to go near him after his close brush with the Spirits, but loyalty overcame fear and in a moment he was down by his friend, rubbing his body hard with the discarded clothes to get the blood flowing through his body again.

"Don't throw the sword back in," Anarhys managed to say, clutching it tightly in one hand as though he would never let it go.

"We certainly won't," said Yrwen grimly. "I'm not touching the thing." She leaned down and pulled Anarhys roughly to his feet. "Put your clothes on."

"Go on down to the village," Cavan said to his friend as Anarhys struggled awkwardly with his clothes, the fingers of his free hand shivering and unsteady on his feet, shaking uncontrollably as though the cold had invaded his whole body. He helped Anarhys pull his tunic over his head. "The Gogarth People might have left something to eat. Walk as fast as you can. You go with him, Dara. Hold his arm if you have to. We'll get our things and catch you up."

Anarhys set off down the hill with Dara. He was finding it almost impossible to walk. Legs which had always done whatever was necessary were no longer responding to his wishes, and his arms seemed to hang uselessly at his side, shaking. Nonetheless his grip on the sword hilt stayed as tight as ever. He was not going to let it go. The blue pony walked with them.

"Put your hand on Blue's neck," Dara suggested. "She's warm. It'll steady you."

With the sword held tightly in his right hand, Anarhys stretched out and put his left hand on Blue's neck under her mane. He knew from experience there was always a warm patch there. After a while he hung onto her mane which helped him walk as he stumbled over the heather. For the second time that day he felt thankful that Blue was still with them.

Yrwen, Cavan and the black dog caught them up as they skirted the copper mine. Deserted only a short while earlier, it looked forsaken. "Can't imagine it ever being a busy workplace again," observed Yrwen.

"The metal's still there," said Cavan wisely. "It'll be mined again, probably for hundreds of years, even if it's not by the Gogarth People we know."

"The Gogarth People must have been really frightened to leave the village that quickly. They're not gentle people themselves," said Yrwen, after a thoughtful silence, glancing across to the mountains where the two beacons were burning less brightly now.

"Yes, they must," said Cavan, and increased his pace.

"You go on, Cavan. Dara and I will catch you up at the village. See if you can find some food," Anarhys managed to say between chattering teeth. He watched his sister and his friend go on together. Even in his weak state he could see that they walked easily in step, leaning slightly towards each other. He stopped, and still supporting himself on Blue's withers with one hand, he crossed the bronze sword in front of himself, pushing it under the belt that tied his leggings at the waist with the other.

"My hand's free now. Take it," he said to Dara.

Dara paused, looking at his pinched face.

"It's all right," he said to her. "I know."

Dara continued to look at him.

"It's all right," Anarhys said again. "The sword's on my other side so it won't touch you. And it won't look odd for you to hold my hand either. Not if you're a girl."

Dara slid her warm hand into Anarhys's frozen fingers. After a while Anarhys added, "If I put my arm across your shoulders it'll be even better." Dara moved closer into him, and he pressed her to him, taking heat from her small body.

Chapter Twelve

Cavan looked around at the abandoned village. The roundhouses where families had lived and laughed, quarrelled and cried only yesterday were empty, silent shells. The streets between them where they had played and talked were still and dead. The fires were out. "We'll just see if they left anything to eat, and then we can all press on across the isthmus. Where did they roast the ox they shared with us? I can smell it, they must have left the remains behind," he said to Yrwen as he set the back pack containing the precious bronze gently on the ground.

"Over there," said Yrwen pointing out an open space where two muddy streets met, and they could see the last of the carcase lying by the abandoned open fireplace where it had been cooked. As they approached it small red scavengers scuttled away.

"Foxes," muttered Cavan. "The Gogarth People have only been gone a short time, and the foxes are here already. Let's see how badly they chewed it."

"Why don't you cut bits out from inside where rain won't have seeped in and the foxes haven't got into it?

It'll still be warm. I know it sounds disgusting, but we must eat something, especially Anarhys. He'll be starving. I'll have a look round the village to see whether they left any bread we could have with it." Yrwen spoke hurriedly, and returned a few minutes later. "Nothing," she said. "Either they took it with them or the foxes have been at it. No leaves or vegetables either that I can see, but I did find some sorrel seeds."

Cavan had taken out his knife and worked as fast as he could to slice pieces off a haunch, and by the time Dara and Anarhys arrived in Gogarth Village there was a pile of meat, still warm and ready for them all to eat. Yrwen scattered the meat with sorrel seeds for flavour, and they ate it quickly, sheltering from the wind in the gloom of a roundhouse. The black dog stayed outside with the carcase and had the feast of his life. Later he vomited copiously.

Anarhys ate ravenously, and after the food and the warmth from Dara's body he began to feel better: his violent shaking had eased, and he found he could control his limbs, although he still shivered all over. "We'll get back across the isthmus down by the sea shore as Cavan suggested," he said the second he had finished his food, standing up and taking on his role of leader again, thinking at the same time that he had earned it by his daring dive into the peat hole. "That way we won't be on the skyline. We need to go straightaway. We can camp tonight in that little belt of trees behind the beach and tomorrow go up onto the moors to find the path home. We can't camp up on the moor, it's too exposed. Down at the beach we should have some shelter. There might be shellfish to eat on that rocky spit where the isthmus meets the mainland. We could go down when we wake up in the morning to look. They're not too bad raw, so long as you swallow them whole." He gathered himself together, as he said it and waited for his companions to finish.

"No fires," Yrwen added, hastily eating the last of her food. "We mustn't light any fires. If the Gogarth People didn't want smoke giving away their whereabouts, neither will we. You should be by a fire to get warm Anarhys, but we can't risk lighting one. You'll just have to keep on the move for now."

"No, we shouldn't light a fire," agreed Anarhys, and Dara looked relieved.

Feeling rather sick after a bellyful of meat they all moved on. Cavan wrapped some of the cooked beef in damp grass, pushed it into the back bag with the bronze axe and sickles, and shouldered it quickly. Rain was falling again, and as they found their way down onto the pebbled beach of the isthmus the wind blustered in from the west, diminishing visibility as the sea's surface was doused with squalls. While they hurried they watched the mountains re-clothe themselves in cloud, blotting out the two glowing beacons on the hilltops. Low tide revealed wet sand between the pebbles and the sea, giving them easier walking than the shingle, and with Blue and the black dog sloping quietly along behind they made good progress.

It's very strange to be alone in this place, thought Anarhys. There is no life behind us except the wild foxes in the village, and nothing but sea on both sides. We can't even see the beacons on the mountains now. We might be quite alone in the land. The nearest human beings we know of are at Ddu village, two days' walk away. When we get there it will only be another day and then we'll be home. Father will be pleased to see us, and we have the sickles ready for the harvest in a few weeks' time. I know Yrwen will miss the cows we traded with Owain, but it can't be helped, and at least there will be two less cattle for the village to feed this winter. With the sword still at his side he walked on, keeping his thoughts to himself.

It wouldn't have been easy to have any conversation: although the tide was well out the waves were roaring onto the sand. The air was full of salt water, clinging to their hair and clothes, finding its way into their noses and mouths and hanging on their eyelashes. The pony's blue coat became damp and sleek, and every now and again she stopped to shake. The sea birds screeched hollowly above the wind under the blackening clouds. As they came to the end of the strip of land that joined the Gogarth Headland to the mainland the beach curved round towards the south. This was the direction they needed to go, but the path that would take them home was up on the moors. For now they headed for the line of cover at the top of the strand. It was nothing much – a few scrubby hazel bushes standing barely as high as Anarhys and Cavan.

"It'll have to do as a campsite," said Anarhys. "Nobody could see us from the sea if we keep our heads down."

Cavan put down the leather back bag with relief. "Thank goodness," he said. "This stuff's getting heavier by the moment. And we've got more than two days to go. You wouldn't think that two working sickles and an axe would weigh so much."

"There's the food as well, but it's your axe that's heavy, Dara," Yrwen said, thinking of Cavan's sore shoulders. "Maybe you should be the next person to carry the bag," she added a little unkindly.

Dara looked at her oddly, saying nothing, then her eyes turned to Anarhys. He was feeling for the sword. He slid it out of his belt and held it across the palms of his hands to inspect it. It was a graceful piece of artistry, and lay perfectly balanced between his hands, cold and glittering. Handle and shaft were both bronze, the handle decorated with curves and ridges, the shaft leaf-shaped, flawlessly curved, and ending in a pointed tip that would do credit to the best weapon-maker ever. But it was evident to him that it was no weapon for fighting. This sword had had many extra hours invested in its making, and it wasn't destined to be damaged in any form of aggression: it had been made solely for some wealthy person to purchase and offer to the mighty Spirits.

Dara, Cavan and Yrwen stood well back and watched warily.

"It's all right," he said to them. "It's just a sword."

"It belongs to the Spirits," Yrwen said. "They won't be happy with you."

"Nothing will happen," replied Anarhys confidently.

"What are you going to do with it?" Cavan wanted to know.

"Keep it. We may need to protect ourselves with it."

"You must give it back to the Spirits."

"No, you don't understand," said Anarhys. "What do you think the Spirits can do with offerings once we've thrown them in the water? Nothing. They can't use them.

The offerings sink to the bottom and lie there in the mud, no good to anybody. They will be there forever, wonderful bronze objects forgotten and unappreciated."

It was Dara, who came to look at it first; Dara who saw things in a different light from most people. In her logical way she could appreciate Anarhys' reasoning in treating a holy offering in this way. She couldn't bring herself to touch the sword, because from the day she was born her family had taught her to treat the Spirits with awe and respect, but she could understand why Anarhys was saying that the sword alone couldn't harm her, and that because the Spirits were intangible it was impossible for Them to use it. The sword was just an object. She came up close and peered at it lying in Anarhys' hands.

"It's a masterpiece," she said. "And so sharp."

"I'm keeping it," Anarhys said firmly. "Whether Cavan and Yrwen like it or not. Don't try to talk me out of it."

"All right" said Cavan. "It's your decision. But I hope the Spirits know that the rest of us had nothing to do with it." He respected this new, confident Anarhys, but had decided to have nothing to do with the sword. His father had been a spiritual leader, and Cavan followed loyally in his footsteps.

"We need to get find shelter from the rain," went on Anarhys. "We'll put our stuff under the bushes. Then we shall just have to rest here overnight, and in the morning we'll get up onto the moors and find the pathway home."

"Can't see much of the sea with that seaspray." Yrwen said, thinking of something to say to overcome a temptation to keep nagging away at Anarhys about the sword.

"We should still keep watch," Dara suggested. "You never know."

★★★

When Grey Wolf and his crews had finished their work at Gwrtheyrn they loaded their boats with cargo. Then they turned their bows north again and followed the rocky coast.

The boats lay deeper in the water with the extra weight. Grey Wolf looked over his bounty. They had taken three slaves, and allotted one to each of three of his boats. He hadn't really come for slaves, but these might be useful if they found somewhere to settle for a time. The one on his ship was a boy sitting in the bows, tied to his bench with knotted ropes, head down; with light shoulder-length hair and smaller bones he was clearly of a different race of people from his own tall, dark Celtic men. In the bottom of the boat were sides of beef from the stolen village cattle, and stores of barley, protected from the water in leather sacks.

"We shall need to replace the rivets of the ships when we land, Grey Wolf," his second-in-command told him as they continued their journey north along the coast. Their language was a form of Celtic which would have been incomprehensible to the natives of Wales at that time. To the boy sitting at the front of the boat it was simply a stream of sounds.

"Right," said the captain, and checked them himself. Sure enough the iron rivets holding the timber boarding together had started to corrode in the salt water and would soon be working loose. "We need bog iron to make new ones, it's easy to find in the streams and it doesn't rust away so quickly in the water as mined iron. It's the best thing. We keep going until we see peaty land, then look for a spot to make camp and stay long enough to find it. We can forge new rivets for the boats before we move on. Continue north, Ronan." Iron was one thing they had not found at the village they had just raided. It was a very important part of their quest.

The flotilla turned, sailing north-east now along the coast of Lleyn. Here the mountains plunged almost vertically into the sea. Grey Wolf scanned his eyes continually along the coast as the June sun began its downward journey in the western sky. He saw the landscape begin to alter, then the Bronze Age people's holy island of Mon coming out of the mist towards them on the left. He saw the narrow strait that lay between Mon and the mainland. Here was a decision to make: either they attempted a passage through the strait with the island on their left, and the coast on their right; or they made a long detour and sailed all the way round the island. This would take extra time, and darkness was starting to fall.

"Sail through the strait," he instructed Ronan, his second-in-command. It was only when he arrived at its entrance that he saw how treacherous the waters through it were going to be. There was no changing his mind and turning back now though. That would show weakness. He would rather die than do that. They would be professional and sail through it.

"Yes, Grey Wolf," responded Ronan, and following his commander's instruction, he set sail for it without a qualm. By now they could both see the dangers. Flat rocks broke the surface at times, sometimes the sea washed over them, rendering them invisible; the water was full of eddies and whirlpools, in other places deceptively flat. There were sandbanks. Grey Wolf went into the bow where the slave was tied to get a better view of the water. He glanced back to check the rest of his fleet had followed and saw that the other four ships were close behind him. Their crews had complete faith in him. Some of them were his family and friends and he needed to get them all through safely. His brother was captain of the second boat, and two sons crewed another.

Had the local Bronze Age people been watching their passage through the strait they would have admired the foreign sailors for their courage in sailing through these treacherous waters. More importantly they would have been quite certain that all five boats would be lost, and that would have been the end of the invaders. They would have been very surprised and horrified to see all five boats sail safely out again into the open sea, but his was exactly what happened. The little flotilla came bravely out of the strait, and Grey Wolf, standing again in the stern, saw through the mist the outline of the Gogarth Head, a dark hump against the grey of the sea and sky. It looked promising. He pointed it out to Ronan.

On the open sea the wind picked up again. "Make for that headland," Grey Wolf instructed, and the boat raced forward as the wind filled the single square sail. There were no local people to see them arrive on the Gogarth Headland. The village tribe had already decamped, and Anarhys and his group, sheltering near the beach with no fire to give them away, could not see far enough through the mist to detect the Celtic ships as they flew past. Grey Wolf could see nowhere to land, so he took his boats round to the other side of the headland. When they found themselves facing into the wind, the crews let down their sails and rowed, and they landed on the opposite side of the isthmus to Anarhys and his group before darkness fell.

"I'll take two men and do a recce," Grey Wolf said to Ronan when the boats had been pulled up the beach. "Wait here," and three stalwart men set off up towards the deserted Gogarth village, leaving the rest of the crew and the slaves on the beach. The slaves, two women and a boy, all from Anarhys' village, were in a state of shock, and seemed unable to think for themselves. They were left in the beached boats, still tied to their seats.

"Nobody here," said one man to Grey Wolf wonderingly. "Do you think they knew we were coming?"

"Certain of it," said Grey Wolf. "Better that way. Having a reputation like ours that goes before us saves us the trouble of taking the village from them. The tribes leave before we arrive. Pity they didn't leave more food for us, though; they've taken everything they could carry."

"There's dried peat in the houses, stacked ready for the winter," remarked the other man, after he had searched inside the roundhouses.

"Go down to the boats and get everybody up here," Grey Wolf ordered. "Get a fire going. I'll go up to the top of the headland and have a look round." He trusted the men to follow orders implicitly. They did: the consequence of mutiny was death. He needed time alone to think and plan. At sea there wasn't much time to think of anything except the next few moments.

There was a track leading the way up the headland, but in case there might be somebody lying in wait for him on it, and priding himself on being a shrewd Celt, Grey Wolf avoided it, choosing instead his own path through the heather to the top. This was how he missed seeing the copper mine on his ascent. The wind increased as he climbed, and the rain swept across the land in heavy squalls. He was pleased to see the boggy land, that his hunch had been correct, and there could well be bog iron here. Cresting the rise he looked about. He saw the same view Anarhys, Cavan, Dara and Yrwen had seen earlier in the day, although now dusk was falling quickly and the rain was closing in, making the visibility worse. He could not see the mountains, and barely any of the sea, but in the near-darkness he just made out the spit of rock reaching out from the beach where Anarhys and his companions were hoping to look for breakfast the next morning.

Despite the rain Grey Wolf was enjoying himself in the empty landscape, and the feeling of being a new ruler over all he surveyed. He was even more pleased when he came across the abandoned copper mine on his way back to the village. With the discarded pieces of copper and bright green malachite ore lying on the floor of the depression in the ground, the broken casts, the furnace house, the water for cooling, the mine openings, he knew immediately what he was looking at.

He stood on the lip of the depression, feeling very satisfied indeed. He thought to himself: here is a place where there is everything we need. There is running water, metals, peat for both bog iron and fuel. We would see other invaders coming and the steep cliffs would protect us from them. There isn't much food at the moment, but we could appropriate sheep and cattle, and the barley sown in the fields will ripen if we get some sun. There is shelter already in the deserted village. It would be a good place to look in the surrounding countryside for pure iron.

Grey Wolf felt very much that he wanted to stay here for a good long time. He descended to the mine head, and put his head into the dark mine entrances, making plans to return the next day with tallow candles to inspect the passages. As he walked slowly down to the village in near-darkness he thought about the one thing that was missing.

Women. A settlement needed women. He had left his wife and young children in Brittany, but they were too far away to matter. He was tired of living on half-cooked meat and a few leaves because there wasn't enough time to prepare it; females could be dedicated to looking after his needs and those of his men. The two female slaves could do that.

But he would like to be sharing his bed with one of his own.

Chapter Thirteen

As night fell the four huddled together silently and exhausted under the hazel bushes, trying to keep warm and dry, and unsettled by the events of the day. Anarhys was still very cold. They sat facing the sea to their west, watching the black bulk of the Gogarth Headland disappear slowly into the night with a sense of disbelief, and quite unaware of the activities of the Iron Men on the other side of the Headland. The black dog lay in the small of Yrwen's back keeping her warm, and the pony moved quietly a few feet away.

There was little sleep for them in the short June night. Anarhys had nightmares about his time in the dark and wet of the peat hole, imagining again the menacing faces watching him from the black walls, and feeling the fear of being unable to breathe. In his dreams the faces came out of the walls and hung about him, and each time he awoke he was shivering violently again. When morning came he almost wished he had left the sword in the peat hole, lost and forgotten, but when he saw it gleaming dully at his feet he felt no regrets. The weapon's powerful presence made him feel less vulnerable, and ownership of it gave him a sense of strength and authority. But still, it was a stranger to him. His knife, which had been sacrificed to the Spirits in the river, had been his own: it had grown up with him, spent hours working in his hand, the handle had been rubbed away to fit his fingers exactly. The sword and he were new acquaintances.

Yrwen, becoming uncomfortably conscious in the bleak morning light, said, "I feel wretched. I ache all over and my head hurts."

"I feel pretty horrible too," said Cavan. "I didn't sleep at all and it's so wet." There was a pause, then he added, "I can't believe so much has happened. This time yesterday we hadn't even got to Gogarth, and the cows and Dara's pony were still with us."

"Only for the sickles and axe lying here I wouldn't believe it either," said Yrwen. "Just now I'd swap them all to have the cows back here with us. We could have milk for breakfast. I'd love to be milking them now," she added wistfully, thinking of their warm presence and gentle breathing.

"I know," agreed Anarhys. "You just miss the comfort of hearing them move around. But at least we got the bronze."

"What do you think happened to the two boys with the ewes that we camped with last night?" Cavan wondered aloud. "Do you think they met the Gogarth people and turned back with them? We never saw them again. We did the right thing getting up early and trading on the Headland. If we'd hung about with those two we'd be going back empty handed; at least we can go back to our villages with what we were sent for."

Yrwen said, "We don't know where the Gogarth people went to. Maybe into the mountains. That's what everyone kept telling us to do."

"We can't go up into the mountains because we need to get home, and the only way we know is across the moors. We'll just have to risk it," said Anarhys.

"Let's go down on to the beach first and see if there's anything to eat," suggested Yrwen. "There might be shellfish or seaweed on that spit of rock, or on the strandline. I've eaten enough beef."

"Raw seaweed, ugh!" said Cavan. "Still, we mustn't light a fire for cooking. I can't wait to get home for some proper food." As he mentioned home he felt a threat before them. He shivered and paused, looking up into the sky, but there was nothing unusual there, and this time not even Yrwen, engrossed in her search for food, noticed the alarm in his face. He said nothing about it. "Let's go and look at the beach," he said as cheerfully as he could manage.

"I'll stay here with Blue," Dara said to Anarhys as Cavan and Yrwen set off towards the rocky spit.

Anarhys turned back. He saw Dara standing alone with her pony and had a sudden realisation of how isolated she was among them. She was ostensibly part of the group, yet she had only met Cavan, Yrwen and himself a few days ago, and she came from a tribe unconnected to theirs, with different ideas and customs. She wasn't joining in with their conversation much, so she must be feeling like a stranger among them. To begin with she had stuck close to his sister, but now she spoke almost exclusively to him instead. He looked at her small frame, her fine auburn hair darkened by the rain, her grey eyes fixed on him, and felt for her not just physical attraction, but also great affection. She might be odd, with weird ideas about fire, and fixated with keeping her pony at all costs, but that was just the way she was. He didn't think anything was going to change her.

"We won't be long, Dara," he said kindly. "Look after the bronze. When we come back we'll set off as soon as we can and get you home to your tribe." There was a stab of guilt as he said it. He had been thinking that he didn't want to say goodbye to her and leave her with Mabin's tribe when they got back to Ddu Village. He wanted her to travel on to Gwrtheyrn with him.

"All right, Anarhys," she said. "But look, take your sword with you. Don't leave it here with me. I don't like it" She bent down to pick the bronze sword from the ground. She handed it to him, hardly flinching.

Anarhys took the beautiful weapon from her hand. Immediately he felt the power in it. He slipped it back into his belt.

"It can't hurt us," he said. "We'll get back as quickly as we can with some food."

★★★

Anarhys caught up with Cavan halfway down the beach.

"Dara stayed behind with all our stuff. She feels a bit out of things. It's my guess she's missing her family," he said to Cavan. He stopped speaking abruptly, realising he had referred to Dara as "she". He wondered sharply whether Cavan had noticed.

Cavan had. "We need to include her a bit more then," he said easily and without a moment's hesitation. Anarhys stopped dead in his tracks for a moment.

"You knew Dara was a girl?" he asked, almost unbelievingly.

"Of course," said Cavan walking on with a little shrug and a smile.

"How?"

"Not sure really. Perhaps the way she walks or does things. It doesn't make any difference to us whether she's male or female, does it? So long as we get Dara back safely with the axe, and we three home to Gwrtheyrn with our sickles."

"Well no, I suppose it doesn't really. Does Yrwen know?"

"Probably. I don't know. I haven't talked to her about it. There's been too much going on."

They both watched Yrwen ahead of them, searching the ground for seafood. She walked with a lithe grace, a slim figure concentrating on the job in hand. Both men knew her well – impatient and wilful, but honest, loyal and hardworking, and in Cavan's eyes especially, quite beautiful.

"Did you know Father wanted her to find a husband on Gogarth?" Anarhys asked.

This time it was Cavan who stopped dead in his tracks. "What?"

"Yes. He was worried about her, and thought she'd have more opportunities if she moved away to another tribe. The Gogarth People are much wealthier than we are, and they've got plenty to eat. He thought she might have been better off with them. There wasn't any time to do anything about it while we were there, though." He thought it best not to mention to Cavan what Iago had said about babies.

"Well it's a good thing she didn't stay with them, because we've no idea where they are now," objected Cavan. "They might be as badly off as we are. I can hardly believe Iago sent you to look for a husband for Yrwen. You didn't say anything to me."

"I couldn't have done anything about it anyway, knowing how you feel about each other," admitted Anarhys quietly, and he and Cavan looked at each other with a new understanding that their loyalties still lay with each other. Not long afterwards Anarhys would be truly thankful he had told Cavan that he had wanted no part in it Iago's plans for Yrwen.

"Thank you, Anarhys," said Cavan, and hurried down to Yrwen as she continued her hunt for food along the rocks.

Anarhys, left standing alone, looked around him, at the beach they stood on, the Gogarth Headland, at the sea, and the moors and mountains behind him. The land appeared empty of human habitation. The nearest settlement he knew of was Mabin's village, two days' walk away. Unaware of the presence of the Iron Men out of sight at the other side of the Headland, he speculated whether there was anybody closer.

On the other side of the Gogarth Headland, Grey Wolf's men had enjoyed a comfortable night in the abandoned village. In the roundhouses they had discovered wooden beds, raised from the ground and covered with dried heather and skins, luxuries unknown since they had left their villages in Brittany and set sail across the stormy seas for Britain. Turf was stacked out of the rain, dry enough to light a fire straightaway on a roundhouse central hearth so they could warm themselves after their days at sea. The fire stayed in all night, glowing snugly. There was grain and meat from their last raid in the boats, and there would be plenty of fish to eat from the sea. Grey Wolf had told them they were going to be here for some time, and with the new slaves to do the work they could rest and relax.

To their delight the crews had discovered something else as well. The previous inhabitants of the village had been wealthy enough to find time and resources to make ale, and they had left behind three big pots of alcohol when they left. Broaching it had been forbidden for now, and knowing that disobeying Grey Wolf's orders could well incur their death, they left it alone. Some time in the future, though, they could look forward to a very cheerful party.

Grey Wolf congratulated himself for having found such an excellent place to camp. Almost six feet in height, well-muscled, long dark hair plaited down his back to keep it out of his way while he was sailing, and totally self-assured, he swaggered through the village. Stopping at the roundhouse where the three slaves had spent their first night as prisoners, he looked in through the door.

In the gloom of the house he could just see them. They sat round on the floor and looked back at him uncertainly with round blue eyes. He enjoyed the novelty of their pale hair and colouring, although he considered their small stature puny. There were two women, one older than the other, and the boy, who had been sitting in the bow of his own ship. The few times they spoke it was in a strange language which he couldn't understand at all, although he rather liked the sound of it. He hadn't taken any adult male prisoners thinking that they would be too difficult to control. Nodding to the man he had put by the door to prevent their escaping, he put off deciding what to do with them until later, and went in search of Ronan, his second-in-command.

Ronan was outside considering crops growing in the fields. "They won't be ready for a while," he said. "The corn needs a month to ripen at least, the beans another month on top of that."

"That's all right. I'm in no hurry to move on and there's plenty to eat for us all until then," said Grey Wolf. "And I'll tell you something else. There aren't any signs of decent iron round here, but up on top of the headland there's a copper mine. I'm going up to take a look at it. Get a really good fire going in the village, Ronan, and find somebody to cook a side of beef while I'm gone."

"What about the slaves?" asked Ronan.

"Leave them under guard in the house they're in. They can eat when we've finished, but they need enough food. They're no good to me starved and sick. I won't be long," and with that Grey Wolf set out on the path that led up to the mine. It seemed odd to him that the slaves' own village was almost by the sea, yet they weren't sailors. He wasn't to know that the Gwrtheyrn villagers only had small leather-covered boats, suitable for fishing inshore waters in fair weather. They were farmers, not sailors, and they had never seen sea-going wooden boats the size of his before. There was very little timber to build them.

There was a pause in the rain and Grey Wolf looked about him as he climbed. Behind its covering of saturated clouds the sun had risen behind the mountains, and there was a dead morning light. The wind had dropped, but he could still hear the endless roar of waves rolling against the sea cliffs below and the sea birds calling above. Alone on this isolated promontory he felt supreme. If the copper mine turned out to be any good, he could visualise himself staying here for a long, long time, becoming wealthier and more powerful with the years.

Out of the corner of his eye he caught a movement on a beach below to the west. For a moment he thought he was imagining it, but when he looked again he saw there were figures there. He could hardly see them because the colouring of their clothes blended with the sand and rocks, but he recognized them as human. Intrigued, he decided to see who they were. Not bothering to go back to the Gogarth village for reinforcements, he set off back down the hill towards the beach, following the exact trail that Anarhys and his group had gone the night before in their flight from the peninsular. Grey Wolf felt no fear at all, he was just curious, and as he walked onto the rocky spit he saw himself as invincible against the undersized natives of the country he was exploring.

There were two young men, a young woman, and a dog. They didn't see him until he was a few yards away, when the dog sensed his presence and turned to growl at him. The three figures, dressed in colourless, shapeless woollen clothes jerked round to face him.

As immobile as the rocks he was standing on they all stared at Grey Wolf in astonishment, and he stared straight back at them. He was forced to change his mind about this native race being puny. These three were small, and thin from months on short rations, but he could tell that under their baggy tunics they were well muscled and tough. The girl had an oval face, with much of the smokey greyness washed off it by the rain, thick dark eyelashes guarding lively eyes with bright whites. Under a leather cap her hair fell to her shoulders, light brown and curling in the rain. Familiar as he was with the tall, dark women of his own race, the girl's colouring seemed exotic and alluring to him.

Any thought of his wife and daughters back home was banished instantly. They were hundreds of miles away. This was a very beautiful and desirable woman, and it didn't matter that she was a native of the land he was invading. She would make a perfect mate for him if he stayed here. They stared at each other until Grey Wolf broke the long silence. In his own Celtic language he simply said, "Hello."

★★★

Anarhys, Cavan and Yrwen froze. They felt as immovable and timeless as the Stones on the moors above them as they gazed at the man who had appeared unexpectedly before them. To them he looked like a giant. They had never seen anybody from a race other than their own before, and with his tall stature, long black beard and hair, round head, big hands and feet, and coloured clothes, Anarhys wondered for a moment whether he was a Spirit coming to take the sword back. Only when the man spoke did he knew for certain he was human.

Anarhys gathered his scattered wits. He thought – I

have no idea who this man is, where he has appeared from, or what he said. He may be one of the Iron Men we've been trying to avoid, but he doesn't have the cruel looks, the waving sword, the fierceness that I imagined, and he hasn't attacked us yet. I must say something.

"I'm Anarhys," he forced himself to say at last, putting his hand on his own chest. "My sister Yrwen," indicating her with his hand, "and Cavan." He could think of absolutely nothing else to say.

"Grey Wolf," said the big man putting his hand on his own great chest, but in the Celtic language the sounds had no meaning for Anarhys. The man might have been saying anything.

There was a long silence again between them all. The waves rolled onto the beach, the wind blustered in from the sea, the sea birds mewed overhead as the four figures stood together on the windswept beach waiting to see what would happen next. The black dog stood anxiously by Yrwen's legs, growling quietly.

Yrwen could feel Grey Wolf's eyes on her. He was paying no attention to Cavan or Anarhys. She stared back at him, fascinated by his height and looks, but unafraid. She felt Cavan's fingers cover her hand and squeeze it, but she could not squeeze his back or take her eyes off Grey Wolf's face. She watched him as he stepped off the rocky spit and walked towards them.

He said, "Yrwen," and reached his hand out to her. She took one step back, but that was all, and she found herself still looking at him. He caught her forearm in his great hand, and held it there firmly. He was speaking to her, but the sounds were indecipherable.

Anarhys and Cavan could only watch in astonishment.

Grey Wolf pulled Yrwen's arm.

"He's taking her with him," said Cavan.

Grey Wolf was turning back towards the Headland, still holding Yrwen's forearm. Unable to stop herself, Yrwen took faltering steps with him. Cavan was still holding her other hand.

Grey Wolf stopped and spoke to Cavan. They couldn't understand the words, but it was clear he was telling him to let go of Yrwen. Cavan, gentle, wise Cavan, was having none of it. He did let go of Yrwen's hand, but only for long enough to seize the bronze sword from Anarhys' belt. Anarhys tried to catch his arm, but wasn't fast enough, and before his eyes Cavan was pointing it straight at the chest of the man who was trying to take Yrwen away from him.

"No Cavan," cried Anarhys and Yrwen together, but it was too late. Grey Wolf, the giant, let go of Yrwen, and reaching over to Cavan, plucked the sword from his hand, and pushed it hard into his chest. Anarhys and Yrwen watched rigid in horror as the keen point pierced Cavan's woollen tunic, slid through his skin, disappeared between his ribs, and continued on its journey through his body. There was a twist of the blade, a choking cry, and Cavan, was lying dead on the beach, his blood soaking over the rocks and down into the sand.

Chapter Fourteen

Anarhys' world lurched as though the earth beneath his feet had rocked, and he actually staggered. When everything became still again his life had changed. One moment he had been standing on an empty beach looking for shellfish with his sister and his lifetime friend, the next the friend was dead, he was facing a giant across Cavan's lifeless body, and the giant was holding his sister's arm and looking as though he would like to take her away. When Anarhys looked into the other man's face he saw to his surprise no aggression, or even indifference. Instead there was a look of remorse. There were words coming from his mouth, sounds which meant nothing to Anarhys, but which held sadness in them.

Grey Wolf went on speaking to Anarhys. Had Anarhys only known it his words meant, "I am sorry I had to kill the young man. This girl is very beautiful and I intend to take her with me to be my companion. He was trying to stop me. She will be treated well and I won't let any harm come to her if she looks after me and is kind to me. You should go back to your people. If you try to stop her coming with me, or follow me, I might have to kill you as well." All this was unintelligible to Anarhys, and it was only when Grey Wolf looked at his sister with a smile that he had an inkling that he meant Yrwen no physical harm.

"I'll have to go with him, Anarhys," said Yrwen grittily, her arm still held in Grey Wolf's hand and her face white. "If you try to stop him he might kill you as well. Go back with Dara."

"We'll come after you and find you," Anarhys managed to say, his voice thick with shock.

"No, Anarhys. Go back to Gwrtheyrn and find Father," said Yrwen. "I'll be all right. Don't come after me on you own."

"I don't know where he's going to take you, Yrwen. We don't know where he's come from, or who he's with." Anguished, Anarhys looked at his sister; not his familiar sister, self-opinionated, strong-willed, full of life, but a Yrwen with an unknown future, caught up as a prisoner. I must be strong, he thought to himself, changing tack, and added, "We'll find you, Yrwen, wherever he takes you. I'll get home with Dara as fast as I can and come back to Gogarth with help. I bet that's where he's going. If he moves on from Gogarth with you try to leave signs for us so we know where you've gone on to."

"I'll be all right," said Yrwen, and she looked up into the face of the man holding her. His eyes were on her, but like Anarhys she couldn't read anger or hardness there, only a sort of goodwill. Puzzled she glanced down at Cavan's body lying still on the ground, the sword lying bloodily under him, his face against the wet sand, and for the first time for years tears stung her eyes, filled up her eyelids and spilled down her face. The traumas and fatigue of the days since she had left Gwrtheyrn flooded over her, and she gave way to tears; tears for Cavan, for anxieties for Anarhys, for the loss of her cows, and for homesickness for her village. She felt a strong arm round her shoulders, and in utter weariness found herself leaning her head against Grey Wolf's chest, resting her body against him, and shockingly thankful for his strength. She was too tired to be surprised to find herself there, just relieved to be able to rest against this enormous man, heedless in the moment that he had caused Cavan's death.

Anarhys watched helplessly as Grey Wolf turned to go, taking Yrwen with him. The black dog, which had been standing uneasily by her legs, watched them go, growling softly. "Take the dog with you, Yrwen," he managed to shout after her. She turned briefly to call the hound, and he ran after her. Anarhys was left deserted on the rainswept beach.

He watched their backs retreating from him, realising as he did so that every creature who had set out on the journey from Gwrtheyrn with him had gone. He thought back to the day he had left his village and gone up onto Mynedd Carngwch to ask for the Ancestors' blessing for the journey. Well, they had hadn't served him very well. Cavan, Yrwen, the cows, the dog – all gone. Cavan's body was at his feet, but his soul had departed to be with the Ancestors. He had the bronze sickles that brought him to Gogarth, but they meant very little to him compared with what he had lost. He stood on the same spot for a long time watching the two figures of Yrwen and the giant diminishing in size as they made their way up the track onto the Gogarth Headland.

★★★

Later, Dara, who had seen the drama play out on the beach from the security of the hazel bushes, decided it was safe to come out and walked nervously down the beach to him. She touched his arm to catch his attention, and when he looked at her frightened face Anarhys knew that he was going to have to brace himself to take charge again.

"Cavan's dead," he said shortly.

She bent down to take a closer look. "Yes he is. That's terrible. Poor Cavan."

"And the man took Yrwen with him," he went on.

"I saw. Where's her dog?"

" It went with them. I think they probably went to the village that the Gogarth people deserted. Can you see any smoke?"

Dara narrowed her eyes, gazing in the direction of the Headland. "It's hard to see against the grey sky, but I think I can a bit. Not masses of it, like when the copper smelting fires were alight, but I can just see it. Can't you?"

Anarhys squinted his eyes. "Only just. But I suppose that means whoever it is could be there for a while. They won't move on immediately."

"But what about Cavan? We can't just leave him here Anarhys. The foxes would find him and pull him apart. Or wolves from the mountains."

"No, of course we can't," said Anarhys, turning his attention unhappily to the familiar body, now lying on the sand at his feet, blood oozing from its chest. "We must bury him, to return him to the Earth Mother. We can't possibly carry him home to Gwrtheyrn to lay him to rest, and it's out of the question to cremate him as he deserves. Maybe if we could bury his body here below the tide line the sea would wash away the traces of blood, and scavengers wouldn't be able to find him. We haven't got any digging tools, but here on the beach we could scoop the sand out with our hands. Once he's in the ground and the tide comes in the sand won't move much. He'll be safely in Mother Earth, ready to be born again as an Ancestor."

"We need to settle him into burial position now before his muscles stiffen. If we leave it until the grave's ready it might be too late," said Dara, remembering funeral rites her tribe carried out in her village.

"Yes, we do. Help me with him, Dara," said Anarhys, and they both knelt by Cavan's still form. They didn't need to discuss what to do: although their villages were unconnected geographically, burial rites in those times were the same throughout the land. Slowly the bronze sword was eased from his body, washed gently in the sea, and laid on the sand. Sticky dark blood emanated from the wound in the chest, and fell to the ground. They pushed the edges of skin together until the blood stopped and the wound closed. Together they turned the body slowly onto its side, built a small mound of sand, hollowed out on top, and lovingly pillowed the side of Cavan's head on it, closing his eyes as they did so. Gently they bent his still-warm legs at the hips and knees until they were lying close by his torso, and taking his arms, crossed them over his chest, palms down. He was in the foetal position, just as he would have been in his mother's womb before he was born. Now, only twenty years later, he was waiting to be lowered into his grave.

"He'll lie in Mother Earth ready to be born again." Dara repeated Anarhys' words, as she looked down on Cavan.

Getting to his feet Anarhys marked out an oval in the sand big enough to take the body. "Perhaps we could use the sickles and axe to help us dig," he said to Dara.

"Yes, of course," she said, and went back up the beach to fetch them. Blue followed her back to Anarhys, and she stroked the mare's neck to give herself comfort before they started to dig.

The metal, alive in their hands, helped to cut into the sand but they had to drag it out with their hands. They would have to dig a grave deep enough to cover Cavan's body completely, and for it to lie comfortably without the bones being pushed out of alignment. They worked together sadly but companionably as the sun rose towards its zenith behind its mask of cloud. The tide receded and began its creep up the beach again. The grave grew deeper and the sand grew courser, until they were having to reach down and scoop up wet gravel, and water was seeping in to fill the space at the bottom. In it they scraped up another hollow pillow for Cavan's head to rest on. The encroaching tide was starting to lap round their heels as they dug.

"Enough," said Anarhys, watching water around them with dismay. It was as though it entered every part of their lives. "Cavan can go in here now. We can't do any more. Let's lift him in."

Cavan hadn't been a big man, and he carried no extra flesh. Rigor mortis had set in and it was not difficult for the two of them to lower him deferentially into his resting place, facing east towards sunrise. Dara picked up his leather hat from the ground, and pressed it onto his wet hair. They smoothed his woollen clothes over his still body.

"I don't like to think of him lying there in the cold and wet," said Anarhys.

"But he's dead," said Dara surprisingly. "He can't feel it. He can't feel anything."

"Oh I know. But he was my best friend. It seems so wrong to leave him here."

"There's nothing in the grave with him," Dara pointed out. "He'll be born again in next World of the Ancestors without anything to go with him. Let's put his knife beside him."

"All right," said Anarhys, and watched as Dara slipped Cavan's lovely little knife out from his belt and put it against his body.

"I'll collect some shells," she added, warming to the task of ensuring Cavan didn't go into the World of the Ancestors empty-handed. She walked up the beach, searching for something that Cavan would not be ashamed to take with him. She found pink cockle shells, pairs of razor shells with their ivory white interiors, blue mussels with pearly centres. Piercing holes in their centres with her knife, she took a slender leather thread from her waist and with small fingers threaded them along it. Leaning down into the grave she wove them around his hands. Anarhys watched, grateful for Dara's attention to his dead friend's body.

"I can find some pebbles for his feet," he said, and looked around on the damp sand. There was white quartz, threaded with silver, and gleaming with moisture, sharp, deep blue silicates, cumulative stones with stripes and patterns, translucent orange pebbles. He took them into his hand and spread them at Cavan's feet.

"He looks better now," Dara said. "Content. Let's cover him up before the tide comes in any further. It's coming over the edge of the grave already."

In silence they pushed the heavy sand into Cavan's resting place and covered him up. Anarhys found himself saying goodbye to his friend with every load as his body disappeared. At last the job was done, and he and Dara stood in the sea which now covered their ankles.

"He was a very spiritual person, wasn't he?" said Dara.

"Yes he was. He understood the Spirit World better than anybody else in the village. Sometimes he knew what was going to happen before it did. He was wise, too, even though he was young. He learned so much from his father. I don't know how our tribe will manage without him. There's nobody left who's in touch with the Spirits the way he was."

"Somebody else will take his place," said Dara comfortingly. "You don't know who it might be. If there are children in your tribe it may be one of them. Or someone might appear unexpectedly in the village. The Ancestors wouldn't let your village be without a wise person."

"Perhaps," said Anarhys, thinking back to the youngsters in the village, and wondering if there was a possibility one of them knew anything of Cavan's ways. He did not know then that one of the children was already on Gogarth as a prisoner of Grey Wolf, and the others were facing an uncertain future since the Iron Men's raid on Gwrtheyrn. They turned to make their way up the beach, picking up the sickles, axe and sword from the sands, and with Blue following, climbed wearily back to the hazel bushes where they had spent the night. They sat close together, waiting for their strength to return so they could set off again on their journey, and looking at the lustrous metal objects lying alive at their feet.

"We have the bronze," said Anarhys. "You've got your axe and I've got my sickles. There's the sword. And there's Blue," said Anarhys, counting their blessings.

"And we've got each other," Dara reminded him invitingly.

"Oh yes," he said and put his arm round her, just as Grey Wolf had put his arm round Yrwen much, much earlier that morning. Despite her thinness, Dara fitted warmly and comfortably against him.

★★★

The brightness of the sun behind the clouds was moving quickly towards the western horizon before Anarhys and Dara, still sitting companionably together, decided reluctantly to make preparations for pressing on with their journey. Anarhys' eyes were drawn unwillingly to the bronze sword lying at his feet on the wet earth. Glowing with life it seemed to be mocking him for being the instrument of Cavan's death.

"We won't take the sword with us," he said in the end. "It's just one more heavy thing to carry, and now it's killed Cavan I can't bear to look at it. If I hadn't taken it from its place in the peat hole Cavan would still be here with us. He didn't want me to do it. It wouldn't have made any difference to Yrwen being taken away, but Cavan would still be alive if I hadn't taken it out of the water."

"We don't know that. Cavan loved Yrwen; he would have tried to stop the giant taking her any way he could. He might have killed Cavan another way. He would have had a knife," said Dara.

"But it was the sword I rescued that killed him, Dara. He…"

"Yes," said Dara, "I know it was. It belonged to the Spirits and they wanted revenge. I still don't know why you took it."

There was a long moment. "I don't know why either," said Anarhys at last. "I just needed to at that moment. It seemed ridiculous that practical objects are lying there in the water when the Spirits have no use for them, and at times like this we do. It still doesn't make sense and it's such a waste. When my knife went into the river that time as a sacrifice I realised how pointless the whole thing about sacrificial offerings is."

"Don't you want to put it back in the water then?"

"No," said Anarhys vehemently.

"We can bury it," Dara went on practically. "The ores came out of the earth and were magically transformed into a living metal entity. If it's buried it'll go back to the Earth Spirits. It won't take long here, the earth's sandy and light. The Spirits will be pleased and we can go home without it."

Anarhys nodded silently. Again he and Dara dug a pit in the ground, but this time it was easier digging, and the pit was smaller. The sword was covered in cool, damp earth, shaded by the hazel bushes. Anarhys went down to the beach and found two smooth boulders light enough to carry, and put one at each end of it, marking its position.

"If we ever come back and need it we'll know where it is," he said.

"Do you think we will? Come back, I mean."

"There's Yrwen," Anarhys said, his eyes moving to the Gogarth Head. "We must come back for her. There's still smoke. Maybe they're staying."

"What did happen on the beach with the giant man? Why did Yrwen let herself be taken?"

"She was afraid that he'd kill me as well as Cavan if she didn't go with him. She told me not to follow her, but to go back and fetch our father. The odd thing was he wasn't aggressive in any way. When you read his face it was almost as though he wanted to look after her, not as if he wanted to take her prisoner or molest her or anything. And I know he killed Cavan, but he was quite relaxed about it. He seemed quite sad that he'd done it."

"What do you mean about reading his face?" asked Dara. "He took Yrwen prisoner, didn't he? And killed Cavan."

Dara could not easily read the expressions on other people's faces. Her unusual way of observing the world was not only accepted by her tribe, but welcomed, and used to the tribe's advantage. She had already shown Anarhys, Cavan and Yrwen a quick and easy way of making a harness for Blue, and she used her understanding of the way ponies think to communicate with her when she was riding her.

"Well," began Anarhys, then was at a loss. How could you explain reading human faces? It just came naturally to most people. "He didn't look hostile. He smiled at her, actually. And Yrwen didn't look as though she minded going. She was tired, mind. But she didn't pull back."

"He must have bewitched her," said Dara.

"No," he said. "I don't believe in bewitchment." It wasn't until much later on his journey home that he remembered how Dara had made their lame cow become deeply relaxed when she treated it at Mabin's village and how she had done the same to the dun pony to encourage it to board the ferry. If not bewitchment, then how had she done it? "We'll go back home and fetch help," he said, putting it to the back of his mind. "We ought not to travel back across the moors though, anyone could see us from the Gogarth Head. We should get over towards the mountains and travel through the foothills, but I've no idea of the way. And it'll take longer."

"I know how to find a way," said Dara. "There must be some single Standing Stones up near the mountains. I know how to use them."

Chapter Fifteen

"What do you mean, you could find the way using Standing Stones? Do you mean the Sacred Circles that the priests used to use to talk to the Spirits?" Anarhys asked cautiously. Dara's words often didn't make sense to him, but he was learning that, however odd they sounded to him at the time it always turned out there was a logic in them.

"Not the Stone Circles our priests built to talk with the Spirits, like the ones we saw on the way here. No, the single Stones that stand alone. You know the ones I mean Anarhys; we saw one on the way here. There are lots of them dotted all round the countryside. They were put there as waymarkers by the First People who lived around here, long before our Ancestors came. Caersws showed me how the First People followed them."

Anarhys was silent, taking this in. He had never heard any of this before, never heard of a race of people living on the land before the Ancestors, never given any thought to the tall single Stones he had occasionally come across standing enigmatically end-on in the landscape. Had he given them any consideration he would have surmised they were remnants of ruined Circles. He imagined Caersws instructing Dara in this arcane knowledge, and he looked at her searchingly. Caersws must have believed she was somebody special to impart it to her.

"How?" he asked somewhat sceptically.

"When we find the first one I'll show you. If we take the path from this beach up onto the moors, then instead of turning on to the way home we go further inland into the foothills, we're certain to find a Stone which will show us the way. We know the general direction we should be going in because we'll need to keep the mountains on our left until we come across one, and we watch the sun of course, but the single Stones will show us the pathways."

"You're absolutely certain? We mustn't get lost. It could be fatal, and we've got the bronze. It would be terrible for our villages if we never came back to them. They're relying on us," said Anarhys.

"Absolutely certain," said Dara with such conviction that Anarhys was inclined to believe her.

"We could try," he mused aloud. "And if we were further inland from the coast the rivers would be easier to cross because they wouldn't be as wide or fast-moving. They're probably just tributaries higher up near the mountains. Even the river we crossed by boat could be possible on foot higher up. But it would be very tough going. We'd be going up and down hill the whole time, and we've got the bronze to carry."

"Blue could help," offered Dara. "She's strong. I'll work out a way that she can carry it with my leather strips. And we could ride her some of the way."

"All right then, let's give it a go, said Anarhys. "I'll help you with Blue." He stroked Blue gently the way he had seen Dara do it, and the pony stood trustingly between them. Dara fashioned the harness around her shoulders and hung the back pack with its invaluable contents between her front legs as she had before. It hung between her front legs, but swung sharply with the extra weight as Blue moved.

"That's no good. It'll bruise her legs. We'll have to secure it better," said Dara, and without a second's hesitation she fastened the bag deftly so it could not bump against Blue's front legs. "We could use long grass to protect the skin on her back from chafing, but it wouldn't last. Leather would be better," she said, and before Anarhys could stop her she had taken out her knife, cut a piece of leather from her waterproof cape and pushed it under the straps which lay across Blue's back. "It will rub her eventually, but it'll do for now. I'll get wet without my cape, but at least we're on our way home now." She stood back. They both looked at Blue standing patiently, harnessed and ready to go.

"You're so quick," said Anarhys. And clever, he thought to himself. And what an asset she would be to any village.

"I don't have to think about it," said Dara. "It works itself out in my head without my doing anything, and I know exactly where to put the knots so it's all balanced." She wasn't boasting; she simply had instinctive knowledge. She would have known how to erect the roof of a roundhouse with precision, or systematically build a fence without instruction.

"I couldn't eat any more of the meat from Gogarth,"

said Dara firmly. "We've had so much. Let's try finding food on the way. Roots or something."

Making their way from the beach onto the windswept moors, Dara and Anarhys struck the path that had led them to the Gogarth Headland only two days ago. They were leaving Gogarth with its distressing memories, and travelling in the opposite direction. Instead of turning to travel home parallel to the coast as they had on the way, they continued to head straight on towards the mountains. On the crest of a rise they stopped to look behind themselves before losing sight of the sea. The brightness that showed where the sun was positioned behind dark clouds had moved down towards the horizon, and the sea was slate-grey, flecked with curling white horses. The beach where they had buried Cavan was out of sight, but they could see the Headland standing out in the sea, attached to the mainland, appearing in the sea like a giant beetle which was perpetually trying to escape a tormentor. They could make out black spots and specks at the base of the hill which was the Gogarth Village. Yrwen was probably there. They turned their backs disconsolately on the view that held so many harrowing recollections, and moved on, Blue stepping loyally at Dara's shoulder with her burden.

Across the sedgy moor they travelled, making for the trees around the foothills. Lack of food made them lethargic, but they were determined to find shelter before they made a stop. The wind had dropped, the air became dark and still as it would just before a heavy squall of rain, then to Anarhys' despair a sodden mist rolled off the sea, smothering their surroundings in a pall of dankness.

"We'll just have to stop," he said finally. "If we keep going we'll only lose our sense of direction and get lost. I don't even know where the sun is now."

"It'll be dark soon anyway, and I'd have to unload Blue or the leather will rub her, even with the pad," agreed Dara. By now the fog had wrapped around them thickly and they could only see a few yards in front. Among the rushes and sedges there were sad-looking bushes and young trees standing upright and eerie like distorted Human forms. Adding, "I don't see much we could eat here," she began to undo the pony's harness.

Blue put her head down and foraged for grass among the reeds. With a little sigh Dara took out her knife to dig up some roots, but when she bit into them they were brittle and dry. Anarhys looked into the back bag at the last of the beef they had found in Gogarth Village, but they couldn't face eating it, even though they were so hungry. There was nothing they could use as fuel for lighting a fire, and with the cold, the hunger, the damp seeping into them, and the familiar scent of wet earth in their nostrils, Dara and Anarhys looked forward to a long night of sleepless discomfort.

As darkness fell, the clammy air deadened the night sounds of rustling reeds and leaves, the shrieks of small mammals, and occasional splashy plops on the marshy puddles. Anarhys, wondering who would be the nearest human beings, thought of Grey Wolf and Yrwen, the band of people who had fled Gogarth the previous day, even the two men who had rowed them across the river, but this night it felt as though he and Dara were the only people alive in this harsh, dark landscape. The ravaging weather of the last fifteen years had stripped much of the land of Humankind so that the few remaining settlements which had clung on had become disparate and isolated, the inhabitants thinking of little beyond their own survival. The Spirits seemed to close in on himself and Dara, watchful and malevolent. Cavan with his understanding and Yrwen with her no-nonsense approach would have been welcome companions. Even the black hound lying at their feet would have been comforting. But they weren't there. All three had gone. Dara's pony, searching nearby for grass, was their only companion.

They cut reeds to shield them from the wet ground, but the damp and cold leached out of the ground into their bodies as they lay on them. Dara, uninhibited, reached out her arms as she lay next to Anarhys and wriggled closer to him for warmth, and his arm encircled her quickly and protectively. They were too exhausted, too shocked, too uncomfortable, to do any more than lie quietly holding each other.

"What's your village like, Anarhys?" asked Dara.

"Gwrtheyrn," he answered after a long moment, and word gave him a jolt of homesickness. "It's in a deep valley that hangs over the sea. There are twenty-four of us." A pause. "At least there were until Cavan died. There are nine children. My father is the village Elder. We grow barley, and we have a few cattle and ponies. Sheep as well, but sometimes they don't survive the winter. We fish of course, there are plenty of those in the sea. Without Cavan we'll be one able-bodied man down. That's serious for a settlement of our size."

"About the same number as us then," said Dara. "Just big enough for the settlement to survive. We're by the river though, a few miles from the sea. What are your mountains like?"

Again Anarhys felt a stab of longing for home. "There are three peaks behind us," he said sadly. "Our greatest Ancestors are buried on two of them. Then behind them is our sacred hill, Mynedd Carngwch. It's perfectly rounded. In the times when our Ancestors were a powerful tribe they built an immense tower on its summit which can still be seen from miles away, to remind everybody of how great we were. It took years for them to build it, but it'll stand for ever." He paused expectantly, waiting for Dara describe her own village and its surrounding mountains.

"Our Holy Mountain is a day's journey inland from the village," she said. "We follow our River up to a lake, and then it's a steep climb to the Ancestors' cairn. We go to it on Midsummer's Eve to see the sun set and wait up all night to see it rise again on Midsummer's Day. We do it again at Midwinter, but it's much harder then; the night's so cold and long. We meet tribes there from the other side of the mountain whom we share Ancestors with, and celebrate with them. It's good fun. This year Caersws and I left for Gogarth as soon as we had celebrated Midsummer."

Anarhys knew only too well how men and women celebrated together during ritual tribal gatherings. One of the reasons for holding them was for the young people to look for mates. A little shoot of envy disturbed him. "More fun than being here with me in the rain?" he asked.

"No, it's better here with you," said Dara, tightening her arms round him and edging closer. She wasn't teasing him, she wouldn't have known how. She meant it.

Anarhys gathered her up more tightly. "Good," he said. Being physically close to her was all he could rise to tonight, but as they lay together quietly in the thick darkness of the night he became acquainted with the curves and features of her body under the clothes. It was a much better sensation than being with the girls back home at Gwrtheyrn: they were often in his arms simply because there was nobody else to choose from. Besides, he thought, in these harsh times women's bodies are robust, with hard muscles and skin toughened by weather, their faces were careworn, tinged with grey from smoke, and the older women appear ravaged by the elements. But Dara had a gentleness about her that night, as if she really wanted to be there with him, whatever their troubles.

Feeling Dara enfolded in his arms shortened the June night for Anarhys. He closed his eyes and concentrated on her – the bones beneath her skin, the knots and sinews of her muscles, the softness of her small breasts, the way she used her limbs. Even as they moved on the hard wet ground trying to find a more restful place to lie they fitted together easily. For Anarhys it eased the emptiness of losing his sister and his friend. When the glimmer of dawn showed over the mountains in the east it was some minutes before they could bring themselves to pull apart from each other.

At last they stood up, refreshed by the warmth of spending the night together, but weary and hungry. The fog had shifted. Looking about him, Anarhys saw he was among the foothills of the mountains. The dwarfed trees and straggling bushes which had looked so frightening last night showed themselves for what they were – simply vegetation. He realized the Gogarth people had not ventured this far in their search for the timber they needed for firing charcoal. But everywhere around them was wet: water dripped off the foliage, the ground was dark and miry and the scent of decaying leaves was constantly in their nostrils.

"Better just keep going," said Anarhys. "We know the general direction because we can see where the sun is behind the clouds. There should be a pathway eventually. What were you saying last night about using the Standing Stones to find the way?"

Dara was harnessing Blue again, ready to carry the bronze. "We need to find one first, but it won't be until we get into open countryside above the trees. I still don't want any of that meat, Anarhys. We'll have to find something else to eat."

"Let's move on quickly then. We might find something ahead. That way looks easiest," Anarhys said, pointing south-west. He thought there might be a pathway among the dripping trees and trailing wet undergrowth.

"Come on, Blue," Dara said to her pony, and obediently the mare followed her forwards, head down. The drenched leaves soaked their woollen clothing as they walked through them, their leather boots gathered mud and they were forced to scrape it off every so often. The journey seemed endless and remote: not even an abandoned village dotted their way. At times it looked as though they might be following a footway, then it disappeared again. Sometimes they were climbing a hill and leaving the trees behind; sometimes their path descended and plunged them back into the woodland again. In the trees it was difficult to maintain the mountains on their left, and both Dara and Anarhys began to imagine they might be completely lost in the endless Welsh hills. There might be wolves or lynx hiding among the timber. It was a depressing experience, and it was only when they climbed higher up that the trees began to thin out and they came thankfully out into open country.

And there, some way in front of them and rearing out of the ground, was just what Dara had been looking out for. A solitary Standing Stone.

★★★

As Dara had said, the single Standing Stones had been set up aeons ago to guide ancient people through the landscape long before Anarhys' race came to Wales. This stone was three-sided, only about four feet tall, inclined at an angle to the land it was set in. Dara stood by it, resting her hand on its edge to feel the Earth's energy coming through it, and searching the landscape for signs. The mountains were still on their left. The sun was above them behind thick cloud. She could just see the sea on her right, with the sacred island of Mon stretching into it. What she was looking for were the telling marks in the topography of the land that would show them the way to back to her village.

Suddenly she saw it, as obvious to her as if there had been a well-beaten track.

"There," she said, pointing ahead of them. "See that hill with two dead tree stumps on it? Behind that is the flank of a mountain, and it looks as though there's a notch in the side of it. We keep the notch in sight at all times and head straight towards it. There will be a path, and if we strike rivers or obstacles we'll be able to cross."

"All right," said Anarhys, hoping his trust in her was well-founded, and went to move on, but Dara stopped him.

"I'm tired," she said. "And it's so slow. Let's ride Blue for a bit. She's big enough for both of us. Can you get up?"

"Well yes," said Anarhys hoping he could. "Are you sure she can carry both of us and the bronze as well?"

"Oh yes," Dara assured him. "Blue's strong, and she can rest when we get home. You go up first. I'll sit in front of you."

Anarhys smiled to himself at the thought of Dara sitting so close to him. He mounted the pony quickly. Once he was astride Blue, he helped Dara up and she settled in front of him, as he held his arms loosely round her waist.

"Now we're all three together," Dara remarked as she moved the pony forward. Blue was comfortable, Anarhys thought. Although she was lean her ribs were well-sprung and her back long enough to give her riders a swinging movement. When she moved on from a walk to a trot, covering the ground faster than they could ever have done on their feet, there was no jar as her feet hit the ground, and with their supple bodies he and Dara had no trouble staying with her. Blue's black ears pricked forward, pleased to travelling faster towards home.

Despite his hunger and fatigue, Anarhys was enjoying this more and more. His chest brushed against Dara's back, her damp hair stroked his face, his member was pressed against her as their thighs lay close together on Blue's sides, moving rhythmically as she travelled. He slipped his hands under her tunic to feel her skin beneath the rough wool and she didn't demur. Eventually he slid his hands up over her ribs and covered her breasts with them, feeling gently for her nipples with his fingertips. He felt his heart start to beat wildly against her. Dara said nothing, enjoying herself as much as Anarhys. For some time they rode Blue on towards the notch in the mountain flank, the three of them moving in time together.

At last Anarhys said, "It's no good. We'll have to stop, Dara. This looks like a good place."

"What's the matter? Are you all right?" Dara asked over her shoulder.

"I just need to stop. Please Dara."

Dara brought Blue to a halt beneath them, and they slid off together on to the wet earth. Their knees buckled as they landed. Anarhys turned Dara towards him, and this time, under the watchful eyes of the Spirits of the Air and the Spirits of the Earth, their feelings for each other were consummated.

Chapter Sixteen

When Caersws had turned back towards his home village four days earlier, leaving Anarhys, Cavan and Dara to journey on without him, his knee was hot and badly swollen and the pain was excruciating. After they left him he sat down on the wet ground to inspect his leg, and decided there was a tendon ruptured in the joint. He had nothing to wrap round to support it, so he found a straight hazel stick and managed to hobble back alone with frequent rests along the path. He paused at a hamlet that lay halfway home to beg a bandage from the people there and wrapped the knee in wet moss in an attempt to reduce the swelling. A little later, as it grew dark, he ate some of the barley bread and meat that the others had left for him, then rested through the short summer night. He arrived back home at Ddu at midday the next morning, his face white with pain.

Mabin was alarmed to see him, both because of his injury and because he was without Dara. The barley harvest would be starting in a couple of weeks' time, every man would be needed, and Caersws was the best reaper in the village. He could be ill-spared because of a damaged leg. As for Dara, despite Caersws assuring him that she would be safe with Anarhys, he was worried about her. They had told Anarhys, Yrwen and Cavan that she was his son, not his daughter, in an effort to keep the two handsome young men's eyes away from her, but even so he was very uncomfortable that she was alone with a group of young people he did not know. There was also the consideration that Caersws should have been in Gogarth to do the trading with the bronzesmiths for the axe, and knowing Dara's oddities so well he was unsure how she would manage the dealing without him. However, there was nothing he could do except ask the Ancestors to look kindly on her during her time away from the village. Nonetheless, Mabin hoped to see her returning safely home soon with the axe. Menith, his wife, did not discuss the situation with him but she had barely smiled since Dara had left. She had not approved of Dara going on the journey at all, and believed that sending her on it whilst pretending to be a young man was a foolish idea that could well have awkward consequences.

The villagers at Ddu were aware that the Iron People had sailed up the coast: four boys from the tribe had taken advantage of the quiet weeks between Midsummer celebrations and the barley harvest the following month to set off with a net to follow the river down to its estuary looking for fish and shellfish. They had been there to see Grey Wolf's five ships sailing past the mouth of their river on its way to Gogarth Head, and had hurried back to report this news to Mabin. Caersws had limped back into Ddu the day after the Iron People had landed so very quietly on the beach near Gwrtheyrn, and at about the time Grey Wolf sailed past the Ddu estuary. Mabin acknowledged to Caersws that he was relieved the Iron People had not discovered Ddu, which was built well away from the sea, but was very concerned about Anarhys' village, Gwrtheyrn, standing as it was openly visible from the sea. As yet he had heard no news of it. Of even more concern, of course, was the safety of his daughter.

A few days later, after noon, Menith set one of the older children grinding barley for bread and went up on the hillside to check the thin brown cattle searching for grass on the hillside. With the endless years of rain and cold the soil by the river had leached out most of its nutrients and the grass struggled to grow. Up on the hillsides the vegetation was tougher, and the cattle had moved away from the village on to higher ground to follow it.

There were two cows, one calf, and a scrawny two-year old male which needed to grow another year or two before it would be slaughtered. Until then the village would rely on fish and shellfish for protein. There was a grey pony filly grazing with them. Menith walked quietly among them all checking for problems. The potential loss of a single cow was a serious hazard, and to her relief she could see nothing wrong – no kicks or lameness, no signs of illness. Alone on the mountain she had time to muse on how the cattle were the very lifeblood of the village, and how the people depended on them. Every part of each animal was used, starting with their milk, warmth and dung while they were alive. After their death not only the meat, blood and offal were eaten, but the sinews were used for sewing, tallow and fats for oils, the hooves and horns for glues, drinking vessels and buttons, the bones for tool handles, or ground down and used as fertilizer. Cattle were the most highly prized assets of any tribe.

The village still had a few primitive sheep, and Menith climbed higher to look for them. The scent of wet grass and cattle was all about her, and the only sound was the wind blowing through the wet grass. She looked across the hinterland of the sea to the familiar mountains behind, their heads lost in the clouds just as they had been for much of the time for fifteen years, and where they had seen warning beacons only a few days ago. She felt cold at the thought, and hoping she would never have to see them again, turned her head to cast her eye over the landscape.

As she looked down over Ddu village, with the wild hurrying river beside it, she caught a movement in the corner of her eye over in the north. She stood erect, feeling the breeze blowing through her faded hair, holding her breath and focussing her eyes. Forgetting why she had come up the hill in the first place, and oblivious of everything except what she was looking at, she watched for a long time. At last she could just make out that she was seeing the shape of a man leading a dark-coloured pony. Riding the pony was another figure.

Menith knew only one person who rode a dark pony, but she didn't dare believe her eyes until the figures came close enough below her for her to be certain she was really and truly looking at her daughter mounted on Blue. She watched, her heart beating. She was a woman who said little in company, but up in the hills alone she often talked to herself.

"That has to be Dara," she said aloud. "The Ancestors have brought her home. But where are the other two? Why has she brought back the blue pony? If she's come back without the axe Mabin will be furious. I'll go down and meet them and find out what's happened before he sees her."

Menith ran down the hillside as fast as her arthritis would allow her to intercept Anarhys and Dara before they reached Ddu village. Spotting her approach they stopped thankfully to greet her. Menith looked closely into their daughter's face and was shocked to see that instead of the pinkness under the film of firesmoke it was drawn and white. Her hair was unkempt, her clothes ragged, and she looked thinner than ever. As Dara slipped off Blue Menith saw how Anarhys was there to catch her and knew at once that Dara's disguise had been blown and that they were smitten with each other. Saying nothing about it, and trying not to think of complications of that might ensue when Anarhys went back to his village, she went quickly over to Dara and clasped her tightly, hugging her hard. Tears came into her eyes.

She stepped back. "How did you get on?" she asked.

"It's all right. I have the axe. It's in the bag with Anarhys' sickles. Look." Dara, disengaged herself, and stepped aside so they could all see the bag secured between Blue's front legs. She unfastened it and opened it to show Menith the bronze glowing alive inside.

Menith stepped back, awed by their beauty, and momentarily proud of Dara. "You've done well," she said. "But what about Yrwen and Cavan? Where are they?"

"Not good news, Mother, but we'll tell you in a

moment. "We could do with something to eat first. We haven't had any proper food for two days."

"Of course," Menith said, and turned with Anarhys and Dara to go with them into the village to find Mabin and Caersws. Dara, despite her weariness and hunger, refused to say anything until she had unharnessed Blue, checked her for chafing and soreness, and turned her out to forage. Anarhys stayed with her. She stood hesitantly outside Mabin's roundhouse, clearly not wanting to enter the low door, and watching the water fall hypnotically from the roof into the drip trench outside.

"It's the fire," she said. "I'm still worried about the fire. Normally I live in my own little house with no fire."

"Come in and sit behind me," said Anarhys, and went slowly into the round house, ducking his head in the porch. After days living in the open the interior looked snug and welcoming – the fire burning in the hearth, the cooking utensils round it, the sleeping places. He gave a sigh of relief to see Dara follow him in, carrying the back bag containing the axe and sickles. Sadly but tiredly, she took out the axe and laid it on the skins covering the floor. It lay glistening in the firelight, a precious tool to be revered for the work it would do, perhaps the difference between survival or death for the village. She didn't sit behind Anarhys as he had suggested, but kept close to his side, but trying not to look at the fire.

Caersws picked up the axe deferentially, holding it across the upturned palms of his hands, just as Anarhys had held the bronze sword earlier. This was how the miraculous metal had to be treated. All eyes were on him; it was Caersws' moment while he pronounced on it. "This is well-crafted," he said. He smoothed the metal blade between his fingers, and tested its sharpness. "The metal is a good blend, the head is heavy and will keep its edge. The handle is beautifully made, and it's perfectly balanced.

"That's good, Dara. You did well," said Mabin. "But tell me, how did you manage to exchange this lovely axe with the Gogarth bronzesmiths, and still bring our best pony home? And where are Yrwen and Cavan? What's happened?" Before Dara or Anarhys could answer he paused and turned to his wife, adding, "Menith, please give Anarhys and Dara some bread to eat while they're waiting for the food to cook."

Dara and Anarhys, devouring barley bread as though they might never eat again, slowly and painfully managed to tell their story, remembering bits they had forgotten and going back to them, sometimes correcting each other in the narrative. They told of the long walk to the Seiont River, its crossing in the boat and Anarhys' sacrifice of casting his knife in the waters when they reached the other side; crossing the moor; the Stone Circles, and meeting other travellers there; the bargaining at Gogarth, and how Anarhys traded in the gold disc so that Dara could keep Blue; the firing up of the beacons on the mountains and the mass exodus of the Gogarth People; the finding of the sword in the sacred pool; the killing of Cavan by the giant Iron Man, and his abduction of Yrwen (at this point Dara was speaking; Anarhys found himself without words); the arduous walk back to Ddu village with Blue high in the foothills of the mountains, using the Standing Stones as waymarkers; and the crossing of the three tributaries of the Seiont, holding tightly to the pony and finding the stone fording places through the water as Dara had foretold.

Mabin and Caersws sat quietly, watching and listening shrewdly while the history of the last five days were told. Menith worked round the stock pot as it simmered on the fire, dropping beans, nettles and fish into it until the savoury smells made Dara and Anarhys even hungrier. She also listened to the narrative, but with a set face, angry that young people were being forced out of the villages and into danger during these hungry years. Dara was the only surviving child of four born to her.

When the story was finished there was a long, long silence in the roundhouse.

It was Anarhys himself who broke it. "I suppose I shouldn't have taken the sword from the sacred pool," he said. "Yrwen might have been taken by the Iron Man, but perhaps Cavan would still be with us."

"Not necessarily. But do you know what made you take the sword up from the water?" asked Mabin.

"We realized the Iron Men had come, and we had no protection at all from them," said Anarhys. "I couldn't see why the Spirits should want all that metal lying uselessly in the water when we had need of it, and I didn't believe the Water Spirits would take their anger out on me. I'm still not sure about that. It was as though somebody was telling me there was a bronze sword at the bottom of the peat hole, and I had a compulsion to get it. I'd probably do it again if I had to." He didn't mention the prestige he expected the sword would bring him, but Mabin, digesting the story carefully and watching Anarhys as he spoke, guessed what else lay behind his actions. He had been a young man himself. As for doubting whether the Spirits appreciated the sacrifice of votive offerings, Mabin himself was questioning his own beliefs after the hardships of the last years; after all the offerings his tribe had made to the Spirits in an attempt to appease Them he wondered what had caused Them to look on his lands with so much disfavour.

"So you didn't bring the sword back?" he said.

"I couldn't bear to after it killed Cavan. Anyway, it was heavy and it would have delayed our journey back. But I know where it is," Anarhys replied.

"I am very sorry you have lost Yrwen and Cavan."

"Thank you, Mabin. Cavan would have become the spiritual leader of our tribe. He had a second sight. As for Yrwen, my father asked me to look out for a husband for her while we were on Gogarth," said Anarhys bitterly. "I didn't do a very good job of that."

"But you said The Iron Man looked kindly on her."

"Yes, he did, but it doesn't mean Yrwen wanted to go with him. It was Cavan she loved. I found him alarming. But we'll have to go back to Gogarth looking for her. I need to get home to Gwrtheyrn to fetch my father."

Mabin looked at him keenly. "We have no news yet of your village," he said.

"What do you mean, no news? Has something happened?" said Anarhys quickly, conscious of his muscles stiffening with anxiety.

"We don't know, Anarhys. We saw the warning beacons on the mountains but we escaped the Iron Men's attentions because Ddu is some way from the sea and they didn't know we were here, but since the boys saw their boats sailing up the bay we've hardly left the village in case they come back. Gwrtheyrn's right on the coast, visible from the sea. The Iron Men were sailing near the shore, so they may well have been looking for food and shelter. It would be easy for them to attack it. But as I say – we've heard nothing."

Anarhys thought hard. "We have no idea where any of the Iron Men could be," he said. "We don't know how many of them there are, or what they are doing in our country. Dara and I saw the one that took Yrwen, but other than that we know nothing about them. Two days ago I didn't believe in them. Now I do, but they're an invisible, unknowable threat."

"That about sums it up," said Mabin. He looked at Anarhys seriously, liking him, and sensing that he had matured since he had seen him the last time. "If you're travelling on to Gwrtheyrn you need to be cautious. The Iron Men could still be there. If you wished, you could stay here at Ddu for a while before you go."

"No," said Anarhys. "I must get back to Gwrtheyrn to find out if anything has happened there. Maybe everything is all right, but I must be sure. My father will be worried about us, and I ought to tell him about Yrwen and Cavan as soon as possible. Especially about Yrwen. I don't suppose I'll be popular with him for allowing the giant take her, but the sooner he knows the better."

"I shouldn't think there was much you could do about it," Mabin commented

Caersws, who had been listening to the conversation, added, "If he had an iron weapon your bronze would have been nothing against it. The Iron Men have a reputation for killing on the slightest pretext."

"I want to get on home," said Anarhys again. He had an overpowering longing to see his people and his village. He looked at Dara, suddenly realising that he would soon be leaving her. The thought was unbearable. He had spent almost every moment of the last few days with her, watching her, helping her, seeing her work her magic, being consoled and loved by her, talking to her, discovering her body, looking at her auburn hair and worn, lovely face. Yet he couldn't possibly ask her to go with him. The risk would be too great.

He hadn't reckoned with Dara herself. She turned her deep grey eyes to him, and said "Would you like me to come with you, Anarhys?"

★★★

Menith, just about to serve the meal, stopped still, spoon in one hand and pot in the other. The very last thing she wanted was to see her only child, tired and wet as she was, and only just home from a dangerous mission, go on to another place where there might be more danger. She looked hard at Mabin, willing him to forbid it. He looked at her quickly, understood, and then moved his eyes on to Anarhys.

"Would you take my only daughter back into danger with you?" Mabin asked Anarhys.

Hearing this question, Menith was unable to keep her thoughts to herself any longer. "Mabin," she said quickly. "Dara's had a terrible time. She's safe here with us. What she needs now is time to recover Don't let her go."

"Let Anarhys say what he is proposing to do, then we can decide," said Mabin easily. Menith was silent.

Anarhys thought for a few moments. "How fast is

your river flowing now?" he said, thinking back to the last time he had crossed it, when the men of Ddu village had rescued him.

"Difficult but not dangerous," Mabin said. "There hasn't been quite the amount of rain we have become used to."

Anarhys went on, watching the faces around him in the gloom of the roundhouse, "So we could cross the river all right. Well, I should only take Dara if she really wanted to come with me, and in that case I should be honoured to take her. I know she's young, and I should do my best to keep us both out of danger. I hope I'll find my village safe and sound, but we'd approach cautiously, and if there was any threat at all we would both come back here to Ddu. But there would be three conditions." He paused.

"Yes?" said Menith, filling in the expectant silence.

Anarhys turned his eyes questioningly on Dara.

That we go tomorrow first thing. That the cow we left here comes with us. And…that Dara comes with me as my wife."

Chapter Seventeen

"You would like to take Dara as your wife to Gwrtheyrn?" Mabin repeated slowly, checking for himself that he had heard Anarhys correctly, and at the same time wishing he knew for certain that all was well at Gwrtheyrn village. Out of the corner of his eye he saw Menith stand up and open her mouth to say something. "Go on, Anarhys," he added quickly before she could speak. He saw Menith bend down to continue working, but she moved roughly, her body full of angst.

"Well, yes, I would," said Anarhys realising with a start of clarity as he did so that there was nothing he wanted more. "Only if you want to, of course, Dara," he added settling his eyes onto her. Then turning back again, "And if you and Menith agree, Mabin." He saw Menith's mouth close into a tight line.

Mabin said, "Taking a wife is a serious step, Anarhys. As you know it means you will take a vow in front of the whole village that you stay together until one or other of you dies. With the strength of the marriage bond you'll be able to help to support everybody else in your settlement as well as each other. It's a measure of responsibility. It sounds easy, but make no mistake, Anarhys, it takes a lifetime of effort. However much you love each other, however tolerant you both are, it's difficult. You are in no doubt at all that this is what you want?"

Anarhys was beginning to be annoyed that the conversation was taking place without Dara's inclusion, but he said quickly, "No doubt at all," and turned for the third time to Dara as she sat rock-still beside him. This time he asked her the question directly. "Would you like to come to Gwrtheyrn as my wife, Dara?"

She turned her grey eyes on him and he saw they were wide and shining. "Of course I'll come with you, Anarhys," she replied. It seemed so simple to her. She took the bowl of stew Menith offered her. It jumped in her hands as Menith started at her words.

"Why don't you," Menith suggested hopefully to Anarhys, trying to think of a compromise as she went on serving the food into bowls, "go on to your village to see if everything is well, then come back for Dara if you feel it's safe? Take the cow if you wish. Perhaps one of our young men could go with you. Could he, Mabin?"

"No," Anarhys said quickly before Mabin could answer. "It's too far. I must get back to my father and the work that needs doing at home. It's almost harvest time and when we finish there won't be enough time to come back here for Dara before the Winter sets in. Iago could hardly spare Cavan, Yrwen and myself when we left for Gogarth for the sickles, and even when I'm back, he'll be two people down. We need the cow home. And I would like Dara to be with me as my wife. We know each other and trust each other. We proved that coming over the hills back to Ddu, didn't we Dara?"

"Yes we did," said Dara quickly. "We work well together. And I couldn't watch Anarhys leaving here without me, and not be certain I'd ever see him again." She slipped her hand into his fingers, sensing them close on hers. Being Dara she couldn't understand that Anarhys' plan was an emotional matter for Menith and Mabin. In her own mind it seemed profoundly logical. There was the sound of Menith exhaling loudly, and Anarhys was sure he heard her say, "Too young, too young," aloud to herself.

"The other members of the house will be here in a moment for their meal," Mabin said quickly, glancing at the doorway to make sure there were nobody else from the village listening to their conversation. "Look, Anarhys, I'll discuss this with Menith and Caersws tonight, and in the morning we can tell you what we have decided about you and Dara going on to Gwrtheyrn together."

"Thank you, Mabin," Anarhys said quietly, managing to hide his irritation with the older man. Why was he always having to thank him? A bowl of hot food was in his hand at last, and he took it gratefully. Dark figures, members of Mabin's roundhouse, started to come in to the house to share the food, and to his pleasure he found himself sitting among them with a sense of kinship. The bowls were refilled, and he was refreshed and invigorated. A different conversation flowed around himself and Dara, sentences spoken with familiar accents and phrases, about farming, the weather, the sea. He felt very close to his own people as he allowed the stresses and horrors of the last six days sink to the back of his mind.

"Come outside, Dara. It's not raining," he said, when the meal had been eaten and cleared, and together they escaped the gloomy confines of the round house to go into the June evening. Ddu village was quiet. As ever there were no stars in the sky; there had been very seldom for those fifteen years of cold and rain, although the full moon could sometimes be seen tracking behind the dark clouds. The three stone roundhouses, sheltering three extended families, stood low to the ground with their livestock sheds, empty now except for Yrwen's red cow waiting to go home.

"You are certain you want to come home with me, Dara, aren't you?" Anarhys asked as they stood at the paddock fence watching her. "You didn't just say it because the others were there and you felt you had to agree to it?"

"Quite certain. I really want to go with you. My mother will want to stop me, but I think my father will overrule her. He'll say it's better for the young women to marry out of the village. I'm not really too young and I can't stay here for ever. Lots of other girls have moved away at my age. It'll be hard changing tribes, and getting used to new people, and the different ways you do things. But I'll manage. I know it'll be all right. And I'll work hard and be helpful at Gwrtheyrn."

Anarhys thought about this for a moment. Eventually he said, "You will be made welcome by my people. They'll love you." Then he sighed in a moment of happiness, "Oh Dara," and hugged her hard. He kissed her and she kissed him back unselfconsciously.

Suppressing a rising temptation to make love to her again, he added, "We'd better go back in. Mabin might come looking for us."

"Mother, more likely," Dara muttered, and they slipped back into Mabin's house and settled down to sleep for the night among the other tired bodies.

The next morning, when the extended families had left the house to go to their daily work, Anarhys and Dara, sitting together, looked expectantly at Mabin, Menith and Caersws. It seemed to Anarhys that Mabin still had a hold on his life, and he couldn't help feeling a little spurt of resentment against him, however much he respected the older man. The last time he had been at Ddu village Mabin had planned that he should take Dara and Caersws with him on his journey and he had been obliged to comply. Today he was waiting for Dara's father to make another decision. This time it was about a hugely significant part of his life – whether or not he had a future with Dara.

"We have thought long and hard about your proposals," Mabin started, somewhat formally. "Menith is against the idea as you know, partly because if you did run into trouble and you both died, we should never know. In the end we decided that Dara can go on to Gwrtheyrn with you, and that you'll take the vows of marriage here in the presence of our Ddu village people before you go."

Anarhys felt his body relax. Dara's face showed no expression, but she glanced at him and he knew she was relieved. "Thank you," he said.

"So that we know you have come to no harm on your way to Gwrtheyrn we should like you to attend our next festival meeting. Midsummer has only just passed. It won't be until the Midwinter solstice so there's plenty of time. We hold it on our Mountain some way from here, but if you can get to Gogarth and back as you just have done, travelling that far shouldn't be a problem for you, even during the short days of winter." Mabin paused, smiling at him, and went on, "Now, Anarhys, there's another thing. You say you traded in a gold disc of your own at the Gogarth mines so that Dara could keep the blue pony."

"It's true," Dara said. "I didn't see the disc but I kept Blue. Anarhys traded gold for Blue."

"It must have been a valuable item to be worth a good big mare," Menith interjected.

"Yes, it was," said Anarhys evenly. "And it was especially valuable to me. It belonged to my mother. It was pure gold. Owain wanted it more than he wanted Blue."

"You acquired the axe for us and brought Dara and the pony safely back. It was well done. In a sense you sacrificed that gold disc for us, and bought the blue pony with it. We owe you the pony. You may take her with you to Gwrtheyrn."

Anarhys was taken aback. I suppose now I'll be indebted to Mabin for the rest of my life, he thought. Did Mabin always take charge of other people's lives? I wonder how Menith feels about us taking Blue. He looked at Dara's mother, but her face was unreadable, and he decided to accept this generous gift quickly before Mabin could change his mind. "Thank you," he said yet again. Out of the corner of his eye he saw Dara's wide smile. It made his heart leap. There hadn't been much smiling during their difficult journey.

And the journey had been hard. Anarhys was tired. His muscles ached with fatigue, his face felt stiff and lined, his feet were sore. He thought of Dara, equally tired, but gallant enough to want to travel on with him for one more day. It would be tempting for both of them to stay here at Ddu village for two or three more days to recover before leaving, but something was driving him on home. He was fretting now to get the sickles back to Gwrtheyrn, to see his father and the rest of the tribe, and tell them the shocking news about Cavan and Yrwen. The people would be preparing to harvest the barley and hoping there would be magical bronze sickles for the reaping. He imagined the barley field stirring in the wind, and hoped it would ripen without the sun. It was critical that he get home immediately with the sickles. Then they could go back to Gogarth to look for Yrwen.

"I'm grateful for everything, Mabin," he said. "For your hospitality, for the pony, but most of all for allowing Dara to come with me. We'll look after each other as we have done during these last few days, won't we Dara?" He found he was thanking Mabin yet again.

"We will," responded Dara. "We've come this far together against the odds, and we'll go on to Gwrtheyrn today.

"Then first we must make a marriage between you," Caersws said. He could see Anarhys restless to get home and knew he should act quickly. "If we do it now there's time for you to get across the River Ddu, and if the Spirits are with you, you should be back at

Gwrtheyrn village before the sun sets." He stood up. "It won't take many minutes. The rain's not heavy and the ceremony can be outside. Come, Menith, we'll get our people together. Are they all around the village? Is there anybody up on the hill or away at the sea?"

"You go and look for them, Mabin," Menith urged him. "Nobody has gone far, they're all around the village. I want to spend time with Dara."

Mabin, Anarhys and Caersws left the roundhouse, leaving mother and daughter together for the last time. Menith was only too well aware that Dara was an unusual young woman with extraordinary gifts. It was going to be difficult to let her go out into the world and make her own way. She wondered what was the best advice she could give her.

"I never wanted you to go to Gogarth for the axe Dara, and now you're back home you're leaving again," she began. "This time we might not see each other for a long time. Don't forget that the moment you're married to Anarhys you'll leave us and become a member of his tribe, and it would be impossible for you to return here. With the strength of being married you'll both take responsibility for the rest of his village as well as yourselves. It sounds easy to say, but believe me, nothing could be harder; you've never met his tribe and you may not even like them, especially at first. I know you love Anarhys now, and he clearly feels the same about you, but make up your mind that you stay together. Whatever might drive you apart, stick to each other and look after one another. However hard life is, it's easier to survive if there are two of you than if you're on your own."

Dara nodded, looking at Menith with her wide grey eyes. "I'll remember that. And I'll always keep Ddu village Ancestors in mind," she said.

Menith, knowing her daughter so well, and how hard it was for her to change her mind once she had an idea in her head, could foresee the problems that might arise when she went to a village that was set up differently to her own, among new people and ideas. "Try to take things as they come," was the last piece of advice she could think of. "You'll be in our thoughts all the time, and we'll see you at the midwinter meeting."

"Yes Mother, but I must go. I can't keep Anarhys waiting," said Dara, giving her mother a hug before they went out through the low doorway and into the open air. "I'm looking forward to it."

Anarhys, standing outside and hoping Menith wasn't trying to change Dara's mind about the marriage, was relieved to see Dara come smilingly straight over to him. Tearing his eyes away from her, he looked around, imprinting his surroundings on his memory. Rain was falling, but unusually gently. They would get wet on the way back to Gwrtheyrn, but the mountains were visible in the east where the sun had risen behind them. The Ddu Village tribe was gathering round them, and he studied the people carefully. There were six small children who had survived the rigours of the climate, several young men and women, some adults, and a single elderly female. They all had a sameness about them. They were thin and wiry from the toil of surviving the thankless wet weather, with worn grey faces, missing teeth, arthritic joints; and each was clothed in inevitable threadbare woollen leggings and tunics. Their boots were plastered with mud, their waterproof caps and capes shining with moisture.

He recalled a cousin's wedding held in Gwrtheyrn before the years of wet weather. The tribe had been bigger then, and many of the women had made themselves new clothes for it – brightly coloured festive skirts, decorated with beads. The bride had flowers in her hair and held them in her hands, and her new husband wore leather trousers, painted with dyes. There was an ox roasting on a fire, the sun had been warm, there were larks chirruping high overhead, and there was a great feast afterwards, with proper wheat bread, eggs, meat, honey and berries. There had even been food left over. That would never happen now. There wasn't enough food to stop them feeling permanently hungry. He had been five years old when that wedding had been held, and the rains had started shortly afterwards. His own wedding to Dara was going to be a much bleaker affair. There would be no beautiful garments, no wedding feast, no larks singing, no joy except for his love for Dara. And afterwards he and Dara would not be dancing, but crossing the wild River Ddu with their animals and hurrying straight on to Gwrtheyrn.

Caersws stood solemnly outside Mabin's roundhouse, facing Dara and Anarhys. To one side was Mabin himself, holding across his upturned palms the bronze axe that Anarhys and Dara had carried home across the land. The metal lay in his hands, alive and powerful, signifying a grave occasion. Witnessing the ritual was every member of Ddu village, alert in the relentless breeze and softly falling rain, and knowing that this was not simply a ceremony they were about to see, but a mystical experience. They watched in awe as Caersws, their spiritual leader, appeared to grow in stature. As his stooped back and damaged leg straightened he became taller and more striking to look at. His clothes seemed to fill, his face glowed with animation, his voice became deeper and stronger. His body and soul grew until he dominated the ceremony.

"Anarhys and Dara," Caersws pronounced, his voice riding the wind and travelling round the village, "is it your solemn promise that you will unite together for the rest of your lives, serving your village, and heeding your Ancestors until the end of your lives?"

"It is," said Anarhys boldly, looking up at this unexpectedly altered Caersws with admiration.

"It is," repeated Dara, and there was a long silence when nothing but the seriousness of the ritual entered every head present. The scent of the earth came to them, the sound of the wind and rain, a herring gull could be heard crying in the wind, but the moment belonged to Dara and Anarhys. At length Caersws reached out his right hand to take the right hand of each of them and clasp them significantly together.

"Then be constant, and always united in your lives," finished Caersws, and released their hands. The brief ceremony was over. Anarhys saw Caersws, as though from a great distance, shrink back to his former self, with his bowed back and lined grey face. The marriage had been brief but it said everything it needed to. Dara felt Menith shaking beside her, and looked into her face. Menith was crying. Dara didn't see many people cry, but she knew that when they did you had to tell them everything would be all right.

"It'll be fine, Mother. Anarhys says it's only a day's journey to his village, and after the harvest we can come back to tell you everything's all right. You'll see."

"I hope so," said Menith. "It's just that everything's so difficult now. If the sun doesn't come back soon we'll all perish anyway, and the Iron Men's attacks are just one more thing to fear." She shook herself and wiped her eyes with her fingers. "If you're going, you need to go immediately, Dara. Go and get yourselves ready. Where's Blue?"

Dara collected Blue and the red cow. The cow looked inquisitively at her and followed her down to the riverbank. Anarhys packed the sickles carefully in his worn back bag. It was lighter now, without the weight of the axe. Dara worked quickly attaching leather strips on Blue to give Anarhys and herself a handhold to steady them as they crossed the river. Anarhys looked uneasily at the water flying brashly in front of him. Water was a traitor to him. Its Spirits didn't seem to like him. He had been near a watery death crossing this river before, and again in the peat hole on Gogarth. Reminding himself that he no longer believed the Spirits had a direct influence on his life, he stepped into the water with Dara and Blue. Mabin and Menith pushed the red cow in behind the pony. She didn't want to go and it was all they could do to stop her coming back to the bank again. Like Anarhys she remembered the last time she had crossed and the memory filled her with panic. Anarhys was concentrating too hard to look behind him. He just had to trust she was swimming behind them.

Anarhys' took a firm hold of the leather strip around Blue's neck. Her size gave her strength and she pushed bravely through the water with Dara holding on tightly the other side. As they reached the centre of the current they felt the pony give a lurch as she started to swim, and all three were suspended in the hurtling river, washed downstream just as Anarhys had been the last time. The current battered their bodies, and beat into their faces, washing water into their noses and mouths, but this time they felt Blue get her feet back onto the riverbed after only a few moments, and she was pulling them strongly to the other side.

Blue stepped onto the shingle, safe on the other bank, heaved herself awkwardly up the embankment, and shook herself from nose to tail. Anarhys and Dara landed on the stones with her. The precious sickles were wet but safe. They looked back for the cow. She had followed them in the end, had been washed further downstream, had made a huge effort to reach safety on their side, and was standing shivering with her head down further along the bank.

All four of them were ready for the final stage of the journey, a stage which would take them to Gwrtheyrn.

Chapter Eighteen

The sky darkened as the rain increased again, tearing down from the sky in sheets. The red cow, spoilt by being fed and housed at Ddu village for the last few days, was morosely unwilling to leave her comforts: she walked some way behind Blue, refusing to be hurried. If Anarhys tried to push her on from behind she kicked out at him. Dara, up ahead with Blue, had to keep waiting for them. They seemed to be getting nowhere, and Anarhys' impatience increased as the morning went on.

"Isn't there anything you can do to make her go faster, Dara?" he asked at last in exasperation through the streaming rain.

"No," said Dara. "They have to want to feel better themselves for me to help them. She doesn't. She just wants to be miserable. We can only go slowly for her."

There was nothing Anarhys could do but wait, grumbling under his breath, and aware of the tension of his muscles. This isn't a great start to a life of partnership with Dara, he thought. I feel furious, we're soaking wet, our feet are full of mud and Dara and I are almost arguing. And if it wasn't for this endless rain we should have been able to see Gwrtheyrn mountains by now.

He recognised the landmarks from their journey a few days earlier when they were travelling in the opposite direction towards the Gogarth Headland. He thought sadly of Cavan and Yrwen, and longed again to get home to see Iago and the rest of his tribe, hoping they would go back immediately with him to look for Yrwen. Every moment they lost was too long. The cow was slowing him down on his mission to reach Gwrtheyrn, but they had to trudge slowly along the sticky path. With a sudden spasm of remorse he realised that outside forces – the weather, the resentful cow, the loss of Yrwen and Cavan, even Mabin's power over his life – were threatening the first hours of his own and Dara's married life. He left the red cow to walk at her own pace, and caught Dara up.

"You're right, Dara," he said, conciliatingly. "We'll just go on steadily. Gwrtheyrn will have to wait." He made himself relax, and slowed his speed to hers, taking her hand. The warmth of her flesh comforted him. He rubbed it against his face, then held it lightly as they walked together. He felt better, as though by doing this they were united again.

Even in summer the rain could stream down like this for weeks, but at noon the clouds thinned. Gazing at the sky, Anarhys and Dara thought for a brief moment the sun might show through, and their hearts lifted. They paused, staring at the sky, as light shone between the clouds, and they held their breath and stopped. They were disappointed. Dark clouds drifted in front of the bright disc again, and the rain continued, although now more gently. The path took them inland, and as the cloaking bank of rain drew back the mountains loomed out of the landscape. Anarhys' heart stood still. The mountains to the south, up against the coast and looking deceptively close in the magnifying atmosphere, were his own familiar tribal Three Peaks. Seeing them almost every day of his life their iconic shape had been burned into his brain. The holy hill of Mynedd Carngwch would be just behind them.

Consciously he gripped Dara's hand more closely. The Three Peaks jutted darkly against the sky, their pinnacles wreathed in clouds. He was filled with a sense of veneration and longing for them, for their familiarity, for his wise Ancestors buried among their heights. They would be able to see him now, and guard him for the rest of the journey home. The ground beneath his feet would become his tribal territory. He felt the weight of the sickles in his back bag, and gave up a short, silent prayer of thanks to the Ancestors on the mountains. He was coming home. Soon the people of his tribe would be out to welcome him home again.

"Those are our mountains," he told Dara. "The Ancestors watch over us from them. Gwrtheyrn Village is between the biggest Peak and the sea. It isn't much further."

"They're very close to your village," Dara observed. Our mountains at Ddu are a few hours' walk from our settlement."

"Our settlement is built on the mountainside that goes all the way down to the sea," said Anarhys. In his head there was a dawning of how much Dara had given up to come with him. Her own Ddu Village, surrounding lands, and mountains would have been loved and honoured by all her tribe, just as his own familiar mountains were central to him. To leave it all behind her to accompany him on an uncertain journey, knowing that she had taken the vow of marriage with him and could no longer return to Ddu without him if things went wrong, showed what faith she had in him. He was humbled at the thought. I must keep faith with her, he thought. Dara is coming to Gwrtheyrn as a stranger. We shall have to share my father's roundhouse and bring up our children in it. How will we manage about her fear of fire?

Detached thoughts continued to dance into his head. Perhaps Dara could take over the stockmanship of the village while Yrwen was away; she would be good at it and would work hard. His thoughts took him back to Cavan again. His memories of growing up alongside his friend, sharing food, jokes, girlfriends, work, were painfully recalled, and he remembered Cavan's spiritual connection with his Ancestors and his second sight as being an essential part of their lives. He looked down at Dara close beside him. Occasionally she jumped up onto Blue to rest her legs, but most of the time she preferred to walk. They drank from the stream at an abandoned settlement and rested there, leaning their backs against the bank of a burial chamber built centuries ago by the Old People. Wild barley, descended from cultivation years ago still ripened there, and Dara and Anarhys plucked it gratefully and chewed it with sorrel. They glanced curiously in at the deserted roundhouses with their thatch rotting in the constant rain. It wasn't worth getting the fishing net out of the bag to start preparing a meal. They were almost home.

Almost home. This would be the last time there would be any privacy for them. Once they were back in Gwrtheyrn village making love to Dara would be difficult to accomplish. It would involve finding a time when they weren't needed at the endless tasks, and a place sheltered from the rain and away from other people. Anarhys glanced at her appreciatively, seeing enticement in the slim legs under their clothes, her head tilted back to look around her, her breasts and face with its sweet nose and lips in profile. He swallowed hard as his heart picked up tempo. Forgetting his longing for Gwrtheyrn he said, "Sit closer to me, Dara," and Dara needed no second bidding. Lowering her eyes, she slid across the damp grass of the burial mound and leaned against him, taking his hand in both hers and squeezing it longingly. The clear signal of her hunger for him was intoxicating.

"We'll go on in a while," Anarhys told Dara huskily as he pulled her gently to his chest. His hand, sliding under her tunic, explored her flesh and the ribs beneath them, and glided across her flanks and back. "Take your top off. I'll help," he said, and together they pulled off her cape and drew the rough tunic top over her head, both watching wondrously as the rain dropped on her naked shoulders and breasts. "Now your leggings." Breathing deeply, they dragged the wet shoes off, untied Dara's leather strips from around her waist, and in a moment she was lying defencelessly against the Earth, her skin shining with moisture, bright hair spread wantonly among the herbage.

"Now you, Anarhys," Dara invited him, and it took only a moment for him to undress completely and hold her vibrant body tightly. He was conscious of the raindrops on his back, the touch of her thighs, her stomach taut with desire, and his member hunting for her. The scents of her flesh and the earth combined in his brain, leaving an unforgettable memory of the place and moment. The exquisite pleasure of making love to Dara could never be matched with another woman, and as she lay with him, giving herself up to him in sheer abandonment, his enjoyment was mirrored in her. When they had finished she lay, naked in the rain, her head resting against the bank of the ancient burial mound, and put her arms round Anarhys with a sigh of contentment.

★★★

Coming back to reality under grey skies and gentle rain, Dara and Anarhys found themselves littered with leaves and grass, their skins ingrained with earth from the ground. "It doesn't matter," remarked Anarhys as he reached for their clothes. "We'll be home soon and we can get clean and dry." He brushed the leaves from Dara gently.

"How much further," Dara couldn't help asking as she found her way into damp tunic and leggings.

"The Three Peaks are quite close now. In a moment our holy hill, Mynedd Carngwch, will appear over the flank of the one on the right. When we can see it the sun will move three degrees in the sky, and then we'll be at Gwrtheyrn Village."

"Just supposing the Iron Men had been to your village," Dara asked as they moved off slowly with the animals stepping along behind.

"They can't have been," Anarhys answered after a

moment, dismissing the idea. "They would have been on their way to Gogarth looking for metals. I can't think why they might stop at Gwrtheyrn."

"I just thought," said Dara quietly, "that the Iron Men might see it from the sea and go searching there for food."

"I don't think so. Look, you can see the edge of Mynedd Carngwch showing behind the Three Peaks. Another few steps and the tower on the summit will come into view. It's really circular, but it'll look perfectly square from here against the sky. Then our way home goes between the Three Peaks and Mynedd Carngwch." Anarhys dismissed the idea of the Iron Men again. He walked on, eyes fixed on the holy hill, waiting for the Tower of the Ancestors to reveal itself. It drew slowly out from behind the Three Peaks, and as it did so Anarhys became filled with foreboding. There was something wrong. His feet felt weighted down, his heart fell against his stomach. His skin felt cold with shock, but he had to keep walking because he could not believe what he was seeing. The mountain landscape against the sky was not showing them a neat square of stone on the top of Mynedd Carngwch, the holy hill.

Instead there was something else. Stones all right, but not a tower. Instead there was a chaotic cairn of stones, jaggedly rounded, and spilling down the mountainside.

"It's just a heap," Dara said, puzzled, "I thought you said it looked like a square tower."

"Yes I did," said Anarhys thickly. Then after a moment "It was standing when we left. Something has happened. It's been destroyed. The Ancestors must have left."

"Left! Why?"

"I don't know. I just don't know. But we must get back home quickly to find out."

"We could go faster if we both ride Blue again," suggested Dara.

"But the cow! She's so slow! She'd get left behind. She won't even walk quickly, let alone trot. Oh bother her! We shouldn't have stopped."

"Yes we should. Do you want to go ahead on Blue and I'll stay with the cow?"

"You don't know the way. You might miss the village. I suppose we should just keep going. We'll know soon enough." Anarhys could barely speak from the dread that filled him. The apprehension that had been present during his time away from Gwrtheyrn was nothing compared to the fear of what he might find out next. Time seemed to stretch to eternity as he plodded on leadenly. With his Ancestors gone, there was nobody to help them, listen to them, protect them. The tribe would probably die without them.

"Maybe one of our tribe will come out to meet us and explain," he added hopefully to Dara, and started to watch for figures up ahead. He watched in vain. He scanned the sky for signs of firesmoke, but without success. He walked on with Dara beside him, seeing the outlying fields of his homeland coming into view, listening for sounds of the village – voices, cattle, hammering perhaps – but there was nothing to hear except the seabirds shrieking to each other in the wind. They walked around the stock fence of the barley field, green and shimmering as the wind caught it; but there was nobody there to guard it and no dogs came flying out barking to welcome them. Anarhys' legs became even heavier, his breath became constricted, but he had to walk on. If he could have run he would have done so, leaving Dara, Blue and the cow behind if necessary, but he could hardly move.

As the village came into view they became aware that the air was laden with smells after all, but it was not the familiar scent of peat or wood burning at a hearth. It was the dead stench of burned-out roofing reeds. By the time Anarhys reached the settlement boundary wall he was almost certain that his village had been abandoned, but even as he stumbled through the gateway, he could not believe what his eyes showed him. The stone walls of the round houses and outlying sheds were standing, but the thatch, the timber uprights and anything else flammable, had been torched to blackness. Scant stores of grain and roots, bags of priceless salt had disappeared. There was not a single indication of life.

Deeply shocked, Anarhys walked over to his father's roundhouse, but worse was to come. The carcase of one of the village dogs lay in the mud in the doorway. Foxes had gnawed at its belly and its eyes had gone, but he could see that it had died from a wound in its side. It looked like a sword cut. Stopping for a moment to look at it Anarhys was reminded painfully of the way Cavan had died. Full of anguish he looked around the village. Nothing moved. Nothing was alive. He went toward the doorway of Iago's roofless roundhouse and was met with a smell that made him retch. He was forced to recognize it as the smell of death.

On the floor, just inside the doorway, lay two human corpses, lying face-up. Anarhys, making out who they were in the semi-darkness, groaned to himself, but forced himself to look into the dead faces to be certain. Iago and his cousin. The mountain wolves hadn't come this far for them yet, but it wouldn't be long, and the foxes had already made a start. He checked the bodies for injuries, and saw that again – like Cavan – each body had been pierced through the ribs and heart by a sword. Blood lay in dried pools under them before it had had a chance to soak into the earth.

Iago's soul had gone to join his Ancestors, and it was horrifying to see how different his father looked when his life had left him. Anarhys would never hear his voice again, walk with him, even be irritable with him. His eyes were dry and staring, his beard harboured insects, his cheeks sagged and mouth was open. Unsurprised by the damp cold of dead flesh he tried to close the open eyes and hanging mouth, but they wouldn't stay shut, and he backed away from the bodies to the doorway. "Dead," he said to Dara shortly, swaying slightly. "Two people. One's my father."

Dara gazed at him, round-eyed and horrified. "Where's everyone else?" she whispered at length.

"Let's look," Anarhys said grimly. Already he could see another form lying on the ground between the houses and they went over to it. They stared down at it in revulsion. "It's Gilda. She hadn't long had a baby. Look, she's died from a sword wound too." He dragged his back bag off, threw it angrily onto the floor so the precious contents rattled, and shouted. "How could the Ancestors have allowed this to happen?"

Dara continued to stare at him. "You must…"

"Where's everyone else? What if they're all dead?" interrupted Anarhys.

"We'll have to look, Anarhys. We'll just have to," Dara said desperately, unable to find words to comfort him. "Go and look. I'll go this way."

Anarhys started up the village. He searched on the ground and in the animal sheds and roundhouses, now open to the air. There were more bodies, many of them just outside a roundhouse doorway. He counted the bodies as he went, seething with rage and pity for them. Men and women of his own tribe, on whom his life depended, each one slaughtered needlessly and without apparent concern. He went back to Dara and found her being sick against the village wall.

"I'm sorry," she said. "I'm not used to so much death."

"I know. Neither am I. It's just awful. Our people don't fight – there aren't enough of us, we don't need to fight for land. They had nothing to defend themselves with. It has to be the Iron Men that did this. That giant who took Yrwen – it would have been easy for him to do this. But why kill them all?"

"Are all your tribespeople here?" Dara asked him?

"I haven't found everybody yet," Anarhys answered harshly. There are two women missing. And all the children."

"The children! How many?"

"Seven children, under twelve summers. Gilda's baby was only a few months old. She was the first baby born in the tribe for five years."

"Shall we look outside the village wall?"

They searched the fields and neighbouring land, but no more bodies came to light.

"How terrible. Terrible," Dara said. "Look, Anarhys,

let's wash the blood off our hands. I need a drink. Where's the stream?"

"Over there," Anarhys said, and he and Dara floundered away from the dead village, collapsing on the stream bank, and hanging their blood-stained hands in the healing water. After a while the semi-darkness of the summer night stole over them, soothing their agitated thoughts and calming their nerves. Blue and the cow, foraging and breathing nearby, moved rhythmically, comforting them both. But if they drifted into sleep they dreamed of dead faces and staring eyes, smelled again the reek of lifeless bodies, and started into wakefulness. The nightmares would stay with them for the rest of their lives, and even awake they would never forget the sight of so much death.

"What shall we do now, do you think?" Dara asked aloud as the dawn broke over the Three Peaks the next morning.

Anarhys looked up to the shadowy bulk of the mountains hanging over them.

"See if we can find the children," he said. "Perhaps they got away."

Chapter Nineteen

Feeling weak with hunger, Anarhys looked up at the Three Peaks as daylight edged away. He tried to think where he himself might go if he was living in the village and being threatened by invaders from the sea. Not to the beach, that was certain. The holy hill of Mynedd Carngwch had been desecrated and frighteningly altered, so not there either. Inland towards the foothills of the great mountain range? Along the coast? He closed his eyes, imagining the scene. If only Cavan was here, he thought, he'd probably know straightaway where the children went. At last he said, "I think I know. If the children got away I can guess where they went and hid."

"Where?" asked Dara, looking round curiously.

"Up there," said Anarhys. He pointed up to the thick granite scree covering the nearest mountain. "About half way up there's a clear patch of grass among the stones. You can't see it from here. We used it as a hiding place when we were children. There's even an old shelter up there."

"We'd better go and look, then," Dara said staunchly. Climbing halfway up a steep rocky mountain was the last thing she felt like doing, but she wouldn't let Anarhys go without her.

Leaving Blue and the cow in the valley, Anarhys and Dara started the ascent of the mountain. For once there was a break in the weather, but the going was slippery with moisture, and their clothes, wringing wet, were heavy on their bodies. The path among the stones, almost invisible to anybody who didn't know it, was practically vertical, and every step was an effort. Anarhys inspected it carefully as he climbed. There were slither marks on it as though somebody had used it not long ago – recently enough for them not to have been washed out completely by the rain. He felt a stab of hope, and as he did so almost missed the footway snaking off it along the side of the mountain to the hiding place. He turned and followed it carefully along, Dara close behind.

There were no children to be seen as he stepped into the grassy clearing among the stones, but Anarhys didn't give up hope immediately. Straight ahead of him, across the green space, was the stone shelter that had been there for as long as he could remember. It was just as he recalled it: the thatch rotting and falling in at one end, and the doorway crumbling away so it was now not much more than waist-high. Walking across to it, he could see the grass was disturbed. He stopped to put his hand on the damp, heathery roof and called, "Hello there." Nothing happened. There was no reply. He listened for sounds coming from the shelter, but there was no sound except for the wind whistling across the side of the mountain.

"It's Anarhys," he added loudly, and then he did hear something. There was a scuffle, a cough, and a fair head appeared in the opening. It was followed by a skinny body, and a half-grown boy was scrambling to his feet, looking up at Anarhys. Mutual recognition and disbelief were written on both their faces. Two girls scrabbled out after him, and then a younger boy of about five summers. Anarhys recognized them all. Four of the Gwrtheyrn Village children. Under the grime of outside living, their faces were pinched and white, their eyes haunted by fear. Their clothes were dark with wet and filth, but they looked up at Anarhys with disarming relief. He sat down quickly on a rock at the edge of the clearing, and they approached him warily. After a moment he pulled the younger boy up onto his knee, and put his arms around the two girls. He expected a sense of deep despair that these children needed his help when he had nothing to give them, Instead he experienced a surge of strength that would energize him to do his best for all of them.

"Where are the other children, Hew?" Anarhys asked the older boy who was standing awkwardly by him – too old to be hugged, but too young to be responsible for a group of children. He moved so Hew could sit by him and Dara pushed between them, refusing to be left out of things.

"I don't know," said the boy honestly. "The men who came in the night took my brother, but I don't know where they went to, except when they'd finished in the village they went back to the sea and sailed north along the coast. They'd killed everyone except the children. Some of us managed to escape. The baby was with us, but we couldn't keep her alive. She died and we buried her among the stones. I'm sorry, Anarhys."

"Don't be. You couldn't have done any better. How have you managed for food?" asked Anarhys.

"They took the cattle which were down near the village, but the ponies got away into the mountains and the sheep are still up there. We managed to catch a ewe and hit it on the head with a stone to make it unconscious as we used to in the village. Then we cut its throat. We were so hungry we drank its blood. I went back to the village for a firestone and we roasted some of it on sticks. The herb garden wasn't raided so we ate herbs with it."

Anarhys looked at Hew with respect. "You need to tell me everything that happened," he said. "But let's get a fire on the go first. Is there any of the lamb left?"

Hew went into the shelter and pulled out a ragged sheep's carcase. Bits of flesh had been hacked out, but it had been gutted cleanly and there was meat left on the bones. "We brought it up here to keep it out of the reach of foxes," Hew said, "but we lit the fire down in the valley away from the village and took it down there to cook."

"I need a moment to decide what to do next," said Anarhys, and before he got to his feet he looked around, gathering his thoughts. From their place half way up the mountain peak he looked down the scree to the hazel thickets in the valley below, to Gwrtheyrn village, full of death now, and to where the valley opened out to the sea at a grey beach. The village stream hurried along the bottom of it. The only objects moving in this panorama were the sea birds, as they wheeled over the water hunting for food, the green of the leaves lower down shuddering in the wind, and the endless swell of the waves. Dara and the four children waited expectantly.

The first thing to do is to connect ourselves together like a tribe, he thought. That way there's a chance we can keep going. If we all work together to get a meal it'll be a start. The children aren't sure of Dara, though, so I must put that right first.

"This is Dara. She's my wife," he said to them. "She helped me get home. Dara, this is Hew, the oldest. Sitting on my lap is Lir, the youngest. This young lady is Madryn. And the other is Tegan."

Dara looked at the four children. They all had the fair looks of Anarhys, with slim bodies and faces. Probably they were distantly related to him. She was unable to feel empathy for them, but knew they needed help. She smiled at them, and they smiled awkwardly back at her. It was only later, when they worked together with a common purpose preparing a meal, that they regarded her as an ally.

"We'll go down the mountain and build a fire," Anarhys went on. "You go first, Hew, and take the meat down. Have you got the ironstone? Madryn, help him. I'll carry Lir. Come behind me, Dara, in case I fall with him." Anarhys listening to himself giving instructions, was surprised at himself, and even more disconcerted that everyone carried them out without question. Apart from Dara they were only children, of course, but making order out of chaos was how tribes of human beings had always endured the harsh living conditions. He discovered he no longer felt faint with weariness, but alive with purpose.

Anarhys was impressed when he saw the fireplace

young Hew had made. He had built it professionally using a hearth of flat stones, just as there had been in his roundhouse. There was a meagre pile of sticks and turf which Hew had tried to keep from the rain under a thatch of leaves, and several green pointed sticks, charred from roasting meat over the fire. Hew pulled his firestone from its safe place in his belt and held it out to him.

"You light the fire, Hew. I need to talk to Dara for a moment," Anarhys said to him and watched the boy creating a spark to catch onto dry leaves. He took Dara a little way away.

"I can find out what happened to the village that night from Hew, and I'll tell you later. He and I can look after the fire and you could take Madryn and Tegan to look for food. Or we could do it the other way round and you and the two girls can look after the fire."

"You do the fire," Dara said quickly. "I'll go foraging and see what food we can find. If I can find dandelion or wild parsnip roots we could cover them in sheep fat and roast them over the fire with the meat. There might even be some carrageen at the beach. By now we should be able to find some ears of ripe barley, despite the lack of sun, and we can bake them on hot stones. It's difficult cooking without pots, but not impossible. We'll manage. I won't take the little boy though. He's too young."

"You're good at finding solutions," Anarhys told her, a little humbly, looking down on Dara's serious face, and being profoundly thankful she was with him. He hugged her closely, but only for a moment because the children were watching. "While everything's cooking we can decide what we're going to do next. I've got an idea but I'll tell you later. I need your agreement to it."

Dara kissed him back. She went bravely into the lifeless village, avoiding bodies where she could, collected Anarhys' back bag, and gave it to Madryn to put the contents in a heap near the fire. Then with the bag on her shoulders she took the two girls, Madryn and Tegan, on a scavenging expedition.

"Where are Yrwen and Cavan?" Hew asked Anarhys as soon as they had moved out of earshot.

Avoiding the question for a few minutes, Anarhys set Lir on a bank where he could see the sea, and told him to act as a look-out for them. Lir sat bolt upright for a while before crumpling up and falling fast asleep there. Then for the second time Anarhys told the story of what happened to Yrwen, Cavan and himself on the beach on that terrible day when the three of them had met the Iron Man. Hew listened seriously. Anarhys' eyes filled with tears as the words flowed out of him, but he didn't feel emasculated by them. The look on Hew's face showed him he wasn't being judged: this was a young man who made him feel sustained, not blamed. It was not like having Cavan with him, of course, but he was aware of an affinity between them.

"So Yrwen escaped the Iron Men's invasion," Hew observed.

"Yes."

"She's most likely still alive then."

"Yes. I thought we could go back to rescue her. We can't now, of course, not with so many people gone from the village."

"No," agreed Hew.

"How did the invasion happen?" Anarhys asked Hew as the fire sprang into life.

"They came in the night while we were all asleep. They had torches and lit the thatch on the buildings. As everyone tried to get out of the round houses they killed them with their swords. We only escaped because there was so much confusion. Iago shouted at us to get away which we did and they didn't follow us. I suppose they thought we weren't a danger to them. They made a grab for my brother, and took him away later with my mother and Elwy."

Anarhys was speechless. The cruelty of these people was despicable. If the Iron Men wanted to raid Gwrtheyrn Village they could have just taken whatever they wanted, and the tribe, alive but completely defenceless, would have been unable to stop them. At that moment he could see no sense in all the killing.

"Where were you when this happened, Hew?"

"There were Lir, Tegan, Madryn and myself, and we took the baby and went round the other side of the mountain. We hid there all morning among the stones. They must have slaughtered and butchered the cattle then. After noon we saw them go up the Holy Mountain. They went inside the Tower, and they must have climbed up because they started to push the stones off the top. They just kept doing it. We couldn't believe it. We thought the Ancestors would be so angry that the sky would fall down, but it didn't. Later they went back to Gwrtheyrn and must have loaded their boats up, because next morning they had gone. Tegan and I crept back round the mountain to see and we couldn't believe what had happened to the village. It was still smouldering. It was horrendous. Awful. It was raining by then so we all went up to the hiding place for shelter."

Anarhys and Hew looked at each other, appalled at the events of the last few days at Gwrtheyrn village. Both the savagery of it and the desecration of the Holy Tower were inconceivable to them, although it came to Anarhys that the assault lived up to the ferocious reputation of the Iron People. Anarhys wanted to hug Hew, but knew the boy was too grown up. He didn't say anything because there didn't seem to be the words in his language with which to express himself, and all he could manage to do was put his hand on Hew's arm, just as Iago had done before he had left on his journey with Yrwen and Cavan.

There was a comfortable silence between Anarhys and Hew as they worked together round the fire. When Dara came back with Madryn and Tegan, Anarhys set the small amount of scavenged food over the fire, and collected Lir, who was still asleep on the bank.

"We ought to think about what we do now," Anarhys said, as they waited hungrily for the food to cook.

"Go up to the hiding place tonight, anyway. The Spirits don't seem friendly down here," Dara said, speaking for all of them. Sitting close to Anarhys she was finding she didn't have her normal overwhelming fear of fire. She didn't feel comfortable with the flames, but at least she could sit near it like other people, without wanting to make a dash for the open air. She thought he had the makings of a compelling leader to make her feel like this, and with her respect came the belief that she would be a worthy wife for him. It was a surprising discovery for her.

"No they don't," Anarhys agreed. "We'll do that. Tomorrow I'd like to do something about our dead though. We can't bury all of them or cremate them, and it's too far to take them all to the beach, but we can't leave the bodies all over the village like that. The least we could do would be to put them into the burial position. I know it wouldn't be easy, but surely we could do that for them." He looked round at the others.

"It's even worse when it's your own family and friends," Hew said. "But we should do it." He hoped he would be fortified by the food for his undertaking. "Even when we've done that, we can't stay here in Gwrtheyrn. It would be horrible. And the Iron Men might come back."

"We could go back to my village," Dara said, albeit uncertainly. She thought Mabin would welcome Anarhys and herself – they would add to the working population – but she was uncertain about Hew and the younger three. There was barely enough food to keep the number of people at Ddu as it was.

"That's a possibility," Anarhys said. He too was unsure of the practicality, of this plan, but for a different reason. He was his own man now. He had led one group of people on a difficult journey and was mustering another. He didn't think he wanted Mabin directing his movements for the rest of his life. Twice was enough. "Any other ideas?"

"To the mountains," offered Hew. "That's where Iago told us to go. Or there's a village a long way to the south, isn't there? But I don't think it's very friendly."

"No, it isn't. And if we head to the mountains, we

might be safe from the Iron Men, but there isn't a lot to eat. Living here by the sea has made it possible for our tribe to stay at Gwrtheyrn. So many other people have left the country to look for better living."

"What then?" asked Dara.

"This is another thing we could do. We go back to the abandoned village where you and I stopped at noon, Dara, and stay there. It's far enough from the sea to be safe from the Iron Men, but we can look down and see it, and it's close enough to fish. It's right by a stream for water, and there are reeds that we could use to re-thatch a roundhouse. There are some trees for timber. There's barley there and probably wild roots left from when the village was occupied. It's close enough to Gwrtheyrn for us to come back when the barley is ripe here, harvest it and carry it back. We're coming into a better time for food, and there may be berries, mushrooms and nuts in a week or two. We're close enough to the Three Peaks for the sheep and ponies, and we have Blue and a cow."

There was a long silence, broken by Dara. "If the situation of the village is so good why was it abandoned?" she wanted to know.

"It wasn't for lack of food. Some of them left hoping for a new life, leaving the old people behind. It became inviable."

"There aren't enough of us. We'd need more adults to sustain a village," Dara said, airing everyday wisdom of the time.

"If we could get through this winter we should be all right. There'll be other people displaced by the Iron

Men who might join us, and we'd have more food by the sea than in the mountains," reasoned Anarhys again.

"Nobody else might come," said Hew.

Dara, fearful at the thought of such an undertaking, changed her mind momentarily about Anarhys becoming a great leader. She had heard about Anarhys crossing the River Ddu without help, and seen him dive into a sacred pool of water for a sword which had done him no good. She said, "It sounds like another of your senseless ideas Anarhys."

Anarhys looked at her, taken aback by her comment. The idea of being a clan leader himself was intoxicating, and this didn't sound like a loyal wife speaking.

Tegan spoke up. Nobody had asked her opinion, but she had one anyway. "We could give it a go," she suggested prudently, with the wisdom of living for eleven winters. "Then if it didn't work out we could go to Dara's father. At least by late Spring we should have something to take as a contribution for him."

"We'll talk about it later, Anarhys," said Dara, sounding just like Mabin. "Just you and me."

Chapter Twenty

As the soft brightness of the sun edged below the sea at nightfall, Anarhys and Dara stood on the shoulder of the mountain and gazed at the ruin now crowning Mynedd Carngwch. Dara looked at it searchingly, trying to imagine how it had looked before it had been destroyed by the Iron Men. She felt very strongly that when the Tower was toppled Anarhys' Ancestors would have left the countryside, and that without Their intervention the Spirits would be liberated to behave as badly as they wished. It wasn't a good outlook.

"If we attempt to live through the winter at that abandoned village there will be none of your Ancestors to watch over us and guard us," she said aloud.

"Some of our Ancestors are buried under cairns on the Three Peaks," said Anarhys. "We could see the Peaks when we were at the abandoned Old Village. And when we were up there looking for the children I felt as though I was being protected. Didn't you? So They must still be there."

"Well yes, but you only felt safe because we were high up enough to see there was no danger, not necessarily because your Ancestors were watching over us from the Three Peaks."

"But I think my Ancestors are on the Three Peaks. Why shouldn't they be? There are views all round and They could watch over us from there just as easily as from Mynedd Carngwch. Just because they left the holy hill doesn't mean they have forsaken us altogether. I'm sure there are Ancestors on the Three Peaks."

"Are you certain you're not just convincing yourself?"

"I felt safe at the hiding place in the stones," said Anarhys firmly, "and I would feel secure and protected anywhere so long as we could see the Peaks."

"Anarhys, there aren't enough of us to keep a village going. Madryn and Tegan are only children. What we ought to do is go back to my father at Ddu Village with the sickles and ask him to take ourselves and the children in. It's the only thing to do. The sickles would be enormously helpful to him. And I'll tell you something else. When your cow was at Ddu, Mother put her up on the mountain with ours, and there was a young bull up there. Your cow could be in calf. She'd have milk next Spring. That's something else we could take back as a contribution to Mabin."

Anarhys thought stubbornly: I don't want Mabin running my life, I don't see why he should have my sickles, and I'm certain he wouldn't want to risk his men going back to Gogarth to look for Yrwen. He didn't say this to Dara, but he did say to her, "What if we went back to the Old Village and made a start, repaired the thatch on the houses and came back here to harvest the barley when it's ready in a week or two?"

"The Iron Men will come back here, if they're still on

the Gogarth Headland, to take the barley for themselves when it's ripe," Dara argued firmly. "I think that's why they killed everyone. They'd be able to take it without any resistance."

"If they are still there they'll want to get their own barley harvest in at Gogarth before they come here. That would give us time to come early for the barley and take it before they do."

"What about feeding Blue and the cow through the winter?" Dara asked.

"We'll have barley straw for them. And when we've got that in we can start storing roots and fruit where we can find it. There are only six of us to feed. Maybe when everything is safely in for the winter we can go back to look for Yrwen."

"We don't have much to cook with," said Dara, sticking to her ideas, frightened at the thought of the responsibility of living in the Old Village with four children through the dark and bitter winter.

"No," said Anarhys, taking her hand and looking into her face, "we don't. Not yet, anyway. Dara, listen to me. I want to have a go at living at the Old Village with the children through the Winter. I love you more than anybody, you're clever and practical, and I want you with me. Please help me do it, and if things work out badly for us we can go immediately to your father at Ddu for help. If we give it a try for a while we'd at least have something to offer him in the spring. If we go now we have almost nothing."

Dara looked back into his face, unable to read the resolution there, but now aware that Anarhys's mind was not to be changed. With her singular way of seeing the world, the whole idea of living at the Old Village seemed at odds with her fixed ideas about human survival, but she began to realize how determined Anarhys was on going there with the children. If that was the case she wanted to be with him. She was practical. She could help. And she had no doubt that her husband would turn out to be a great tribal leader. There was a stillness between them: they could smell the wet grass under their feet, feel themselves breathing and their hands touching. The land, the sea and sky seemed enormous, and it was an intimate moment when they both felt at one with each other and the Spirits.

"All right, Anarhys. I'll come with you," she said at last.

The shelter among the scree was damp, cramped, and smelled of wet earth and bodies. There was only just room for Anarhys and Dara to burrow in out of the rain that night with Hew and the three younger children. As he did so, Anarhys glanced back outside. The memory of Cavan telling him about Iago standing in the hiding place came back vividly to him, and he wondered again what his father had been doing there. Digging something up? Something he had lost? Looking for roots perhaps? But there was no food to dig up here. Burying something he no longer wanted? But what? Anarhys turned over so that Dara was lying with her back against his chest, her head pillowed on his arm, and he put his other arm round her to hold her more closely. He rested his cheek against the top of her hair, pondering on the day he had met he, her unusual ways, the treatment of his lame cow, her practical solutions to problems. The rain rumbled incessantly on the old hide roof, sometimes heavier, sometimes easing a little. Drops of rain slipped through holes in the thatch, dripping on their clothes.

Anarhys lay awake thinking for a long time, sensing Dara breathe deeply against him. He guessed she was asleep, and the children too, feeling safer now there were adults among them. Dara felt warm and relaxed, and he was just about to slide into unconsciousness himself when the idea of Iago standing in the hiding place came back to him again, and he was suddenly wide awake with a new insight. What if Iago had been burying something?

But not something he no longer wanted.

Rather, something that he wanted to keep safe.

The gold discs? Was this where the rest of the family treasure was hidden? And if that was the case, Iago must have been up here quite recently to collect the disc he gave to Anarhys before they left for the Gogarth Head. If so the other one must be up here still, and if the earth had been disturbed, he might be able to find it. Not now, of course, but later, when they might need it. He'd have a scout some time to see if he could see anything.

In the morning the remains of last night's meal made a breakfast for the group before they nerved themselves to enter Gwrtheyrn Village again; the task of dealing with so many of their tribespeople's bodies still had to be done. At the village the earth was covered in mud where feet had trodden paths among the buildings, but inside the charred roundhouses the ground, covered in skins, was drier. Leaving Lir to watch the sea again, the other five set to on the task, dragging and carrying the dead as gently as they could into the roundhouses they had so recently occupied whilst they were alive.

The dead skin was grey and slippery, the clothes, drenched from days in falling rain, tore and slipped as they were handled, and the flesh weighed heavily from the bones. The smell was sickening. Tegan supported the head of each body as it was moved, to give some dignity, and each was laid in line with the others of its house in foetal position. Combs, trinkets, personal items, anything complete or valuable that could be found were laid at the head and feet of the bodies, to accompany them into the next world, and hair and clothes were smoothed tenderly over the remains. Anarhys retained some pots and cooking utensils, and rather than leaving them in the roundhouses as grave goods, put them outside the village gateway, sheltered from the rain, and ready to take with him to the Old Village. Later, he added animal hides, which had served as beds, to the pile. He reasoned that while his tribespeople might want goods to accompany them on their last journey to the afterlife, he, Dara and the children could do with practical help in their present life. Nobody questioned him about it.

The work was done. Gwrtheyrn Village, once a lively working settlement full of love, anger, jealousy, joy, despair and hope, was left to rest in peace. For once the rain had kept away, and the clouds had lifted above the tops of the Three Peaks standing behind them. Anarhys and Dara stood together at the village gateway, not looking at what they had undertaken, but down at the sea below.

"There's nothing more to stay for," Anarhys said quietly. "We've done everything we could."

Finding it impossible to imagine what Anarhys was feeling, Dara could only answer, "Your Ancestors will see what we have done and be pleased. If the wolves and foxes come disturbing them it won't matter. We won't have to see them. It would have been impossible for us to bury or cremate your people, and at least we've allowed them to go on their final journey to the afterlife with dignity."

Anarhys nodded, unable to speak. He badly wanted to spend time mourning for his people, thinking of them, crying for them, spending time saying goodbye to them. He was sharply aware that had he not been away on his mission to the Gogarth Headland when the Iron men came he would have been yet one more dead body lying among them. Being able to settle his people to go on their last journey eased the guilt of being alive when they were not.

"I'll go and fetch Blue," Dara offered, as he remained silent, thinking deeply. "We can pack the hides onto her to take to the Old Village, and I'll secure them with leather strips." She came back a few minutes later with the pony. Anarhys still didn't move, and Hew helped to load the skins. Anarhys looked at him working, remembering his missing brother. He forced himself to move, and went to help, taking his leave of friends and family of a lifetime, and taking up instead his new burden of responsibility as leader of a small group of people.

★★★

They left Gwrtheyrn Village together: six human beings and two tired animals. They took the same route Anarhys, Cavan and Yrwen had taken when they left the village eight days ago, not knowing then what was ahead of them. Only Anarhys remained of the original company. He walked at the back, behind the cow, observing the others. Dara was ahead with Blue, Lir perched on top of the pack of hides. Hew walked on the other side, steadying Lir. Madryn and Tegan shuffled wearily behind them, their arms full of cooking utensils.

There are six of us, thought Anarhys. We have one pony, and a cow which might or might not be in calf. There are two scythes and a fishing net in my back bag, and we have a few pots and utensils. There are sheep and ponies left on the Three Peaks, and it's possible I could find the other gold disc at the hiding place. Things could be worse.

He hurried to catch up with Dara so he could walk with her, calling to Madryn to go behind the cow. The air seemed brighter and his back felt warm. Lir, who had seen only grey skies during most of his life, turned his head about from his vantage point high up on the hides on Blue's back, then looked down at Anarhys from his perch on the pony.

"What's happening to the sky?" he asked.

Anarhys, Dara and Hew looked up and around in wonder. The clouds above had parted, and to their astonishment they saw the brilliant beam of the sun's face fully visible above them. Small pieces of blue sky, growing and connecting together, showed through as the greyness dispersed. The sky was clearing. They stopped together, and the two girls walking behind almost collided with them.

All of them felt the heat on their skin, seeping through their flesh and into their bones. As the sun grew stronger, moisture evaporated from their clothes and hair, and they spread their hands out, turning their faces towards the warmth, breathing deeply and thankfully in the brightness. Glancing over to the sea, Anarhys saw that where it had been sullen and dark a few moments ago, there was a sparkle on its surface, and its colour was changing to an uncertain turquoise. Not long after the sky and sea were blue with promise.

"The Ancestors must have interceded for us," Anarhys said at last.

"Then we must have been doing something right," his wife said, taking his arm in both her hands, and looking up into his face.

Epilogue

Grey Wolf the Celt and his men continued to live along the North Welsh coast. As the weather returned to normal they become wealthy farmers, and they and their descendants ruled the area for hundreds of years. As the Celts, with their handsome iron work, increased in numbers, tales were told among them about the original race of small people living clandestinely in the mountains and along the edges of the sea. It was said that these bands of attractive little creatures had pointed ears and magical powers, but that although they could work bronze they were mortally afraid of iron. They stole from the Iron Age villages, occasionally kidnapping babies, or even adults, and if these hostages ever returned to their Celtic homes they had somehow been changed by their stay among these curious creatures. The Celts called the little people "Fairies".

When the Romans finally forced the Celts out of Wales several hundred years later they took over the mines themselves, just as Grey Wolf took them from the Bronze Age people when Anarhys was escaping with Dara, Yrwen and Cavan.

Lightning Source UK Ltd.
Milton Keynes UK
UKOW05f0727190215

246487UK00001B/28/P